The Antique Mirror
and the
Ancient Secret

A Sequel to

The Angel in the Garden

Teresa E. Lavergne

Publishing this book and its prequel, The Angel in the Garden, has been an act of faith for me. I had to truly and firmly believe that it was indeed the Lord's intention for me to write and publish a series of children's allegory fiction books.

Throughout the writing of this book and the prequel, I have been so thrilled to note how the Lord Himself seemed to be standing by me, giving me the directions and ideas for these stories.

I feel that I have come to know Jesus better, through working with Him on these books, and now my hope is that you, the reader, will want to know Him better as you read this book.

Knowing Him better leads to loving Him more! And that is the best thing that could happen to us.

Other Books by Teresa Lavergne:

The Angel in the Garden

In the Garden of His Grace

Other books by Guy and Teresa Lavergne:

Act Upon a Story: 60 Bible Skits for Ministry

Act Upon a Story: A Series of Skits about Joseph

Act Upon a Story: A Collection of Christmas Plays

Chapter 1

It has always seemed to me a very sad thing that the places of our childhood memories do not remain the same, and we cannot go back to visit them. People move away, houses are sold, and the memories become fragile. I think that is why some people like to put a small memento in a keepsake box. It might be only a rock, but it has a meaning for that person.

This was certainly true of Audrey. She kept a white rock in a small wooden box and no one knew the meaning of that rock, except for one other person in the world. But since this other person could not be found, Audrey felt quite alone and singular in her secret.

No one else knew of the strange but wonderful adventure she had had as a child, and she had never mentioned it to another person. The beginning of this adventure had occurred at a certain yellow house, which had a lovely garden and a very old stone angel within it.

She had gone back to this place in recent years, only to discover that the house had been sold. The new owners did not value the upkeep of such a lush garden as did the previous owners, and so the garden itself no longer existed. When Audrey inquired about the stone angel, there were blank stares in response. No one seemed to know anything about it, much less what had happened to it.

In a rather dismal daze, she returned to her car and slowly drove away. On a whim, she decided to go to the downtown shops and simply browse a little before leaving this small town. This proved to be a momentous decision, for when she saw the name of one certain shop, she knew she had stumbled onto a very great circumstance.

The shop was called "The Rusty Pearl"---and Audrey knew in an instant to whom this shop must belong, and her heart began to beat very rapidly. She stepped inside, and realized that she was holding her breath in her excitement and anticipation.

The next moment, her breath was being squeezed out of her by a very fierce hug from a man with rust-colored curly hair. When he finally let go of her, she was promptly squeezed in an embrace from a petite, fair-skinned young woman with jet-black hair and almond-shaped eyes.

As you may have guessed already, these two people were none other than Rusty and Pearl, from the Kingdom of Grace.

Pearl looked at Audrey with shining eyes and said, "I knew you would come." Audrey was so overcome with elation and joy that she could not even answer. Rusty promptly went to the door and turned the hanging sign on it around so that it said "CLOSED" instead of "OPEN".

"We have so much talking to do, we'll close the shop for now," he said. Then he and Pearl and Audrey went to the back room which had a table and chairs, a small kitchen, and a sofa. There was one small window placed rather high in this room.

Pearl began heating water in a teakettle for cranberry vanilla tea, and Audrey had that sense of being back in time as if they were again sitting at Authentica's table.

Audrey still could not believe that she was really with them; she kept wondering if this was all a dream. "I never thought I would see you again," she told Rusty and Pearl.

"I just had this feeling that you would come," said Pearl. "And here you are."

"What are you doing here, in this world?" asked Audrey, who was totally baffled at seeing them in a place she had not expected. (For you see, the Kingdom of Grace is not part of this world, but Audrey had visited there as a child)

Rusty laughed and said, "You know how the Prince likes to surprise us. I imagine that he is very delighted to see this reunion we are having."

"But you are not here just on my account, are you?" asked Audrey in bewilderment.

"No," Rusty answered. "We are on a mission, and this time it may be a life-long mission. We are not sure of all the details as yet."

"We do know it will involve children---but whose they are, we don't know yet. We don't know if they will be our own, or someone else's children," said Pearl earnestly.

"So you two are married!" exclaimed Audrey with satisfaction.

"Yes," Rusty and Pearl answered together.

And the look in Pearl's eyes when she gazed at Rusty, and the way he held Pearl's hand in response, reminded Audrey of the love of the Prince for his children. How she longed to see the face of the Prince again----and to physically hear his compassionate voice. But Audrey carried his promises in her heart, and it would have to suffice for now. His promises *would* be enough, for they were literally "out of this world."

"I wish I could have seen your wedding," said Audrey wistfully.

"And we wish you could have been there," said Rusty.

"What was it like?" asked Audrey with heartfelt interest and wonder.

"It was very much like your going-away celebration!" said Pearl. "The Prince sang over us, and gave us our heart's desire, which was his blessing."

"Then he sent us here, and that was quite a shock," said Rusty. "We had an incredible amount to learn and to get used to----all the technology and advancements in science and learning were a lot to deal with, I can assure you!"

"We had to learn to drive cars, and use computers," said Pearl, laughing with merriment at their awkward predicament. "We were small children all over again."

"The simplest things could baffle us," said Rusty, laughing too. "Like turning things on."

Audrey smiled with understanding, and then asked: "Where---and how---is Cedric?"

"He has readily taken my place," said Rusty. "He is one of the archers protecting the palace, and also is training the ones who have been rescued."

"Oh, I am so thankful to hear that!" exclaimed Audrey. "And Authentica?"

Pearl answered her question gently but soberly: "Authentica has passed over into the Prince's father's realm. You remember that time is different there than it is here."

"Yes," said Audrey. "I do remember, and I will never forget her help and guidance when I was a child."

"That is what she lived for," said Rusty. "And she did this until the very end of her life."

"Saphire now is wearing her mantle, so to speak," said Pearl. "Saphire is continuing to do what Authentica used to do for the children in the way of guidance, although she cannot be a spy in the evil prince's realm."

(I must add a note for the reader's sake: Saphire was once Pearl's guardian, and would always be very dear to her)

"And Cornelia---have you heard from her?" asked Pearl.

"No," said Audrey sadly. "I have never seen her again."

"Nor have we," said Rusty, in a somber tone of voice. "But I am sure that the Prince is well aware of her and where she is."

"Yes, I know," said Audrey with a sigh. "I only wish I had thought to ask her full name back then. I don't even know her last name."

Pearl smiled thoughtfully and then she said: "Children don't think of many years from now--- they tend to live only in the present."

"Well, here I am in the present," said Audrey, "And I don't want to make the same mistake again! What are your last names?"

Rusty's eyes twinkled, and a mischievous smile came to his lips. "Well, if you must know, we are spies, and we have an assumed identity. My alias is Reginald Rowan McAlister, and this is Pearl Kioko McAlister."

"That must have been a feat!---to create an existence where there wasn't one before," mused Audrey.

"But nothing too hard for one who specializes in creating things out of nothing!" said Pearl.

And now dear Reader, I shall leave the rest of
their conversation to your imagination, as they
continued to catch up on all the years since
Audrey's childhood visit to the Kingdom of Grace.

Chapter 2

It was terribly hard for Audrey to say goodbye to her friends, who she had never dreamed of seeing again. Since she was the one who had to leave, she had to muster the most resolve. Yet it was equally hard for Rusty and Pearl to let her go. In this entire world, Audrey was the only one with whom they could converse about their homeland. (Except for Cornelia, of course)

This time, however, they would be able to exchange letters. That thought kept their spirits up, as Audrey walked to her car. She settled in, and changed gears to back away. There were tears welling up in Pearl's eyes, and Rusty put his arm around her.

With a final wave, Audrey drove away from the little antique shop that now held a great mystery and a great secret----though none of them knew how great it would turn out to be.

In the weeks that followed, a rather large package was delivered to the little antique store. It had no return address, and both Rusty and Pearl could not determine a feasible source for the package. Neither one had ordered anything.

Inside the package, they found a large antique mirror. It had been carefully wrapped with many layers of foam to prevent breakage during the shipment. Whoever had sent it, evidently valued the item, as seen in the care and precaution taken for its shipment.

After inquiring with the shipping companies and the post office, Rusty and Pearl had to give up the search. They could find no trace of the previous owner, or of its shipment or even a tracking number. It remained a mystery.

"Rusty," said Pearl. "Do you think the Prince sent it here?"

Rusty looked at Pearl with keen eyes and then said: "He does enjoy doing the impossible."

"Well, then," answered Pearl. "I think we should hang it up, but not advertise it as for sale."

"I think so, too," said Rusty, and they proceeded to do this.

After the mirror was hung on a wall in the front room of the store, Rusty and Pearl stood back and looked at it. It was a truly beautiful piece of work; the mirror glass was beveled, and the wood frame was carved ornately with clusters of grapes.

The mirror drew attention right away, and several customers wanted to buy it, but Rusty and Pearl politely declined the offers. Since the origin and sender of the mirror remained unknown, Rusty and Pearl could not offer any information about the mirror to inquirers. The mystery seemed to intrigue the antique hunters even more.

The mirror continued to have some sort of attraction to itself, when any new customers came.

Although there was a small collection of antique toys in one area, children seldom ventured into the antique store. So Rusty and Pearl became very interested in the few who did.

There was a brother and sister who came in one day, and the mirror immediately caught their attention. They stood still, looking wistfully at it. Finally they explained that they were looking for a gift for their mother, but they knew they could not afford the mirror.

Pearl explained that it wasn't for sale anyway, but she would be happy to try to help them find a smaller gift for their mother. Pearl showed them jewelry boxes, fans, teapots, jewelry, and scarves, and the children finally chose a pair of earrings.

Rusty was repairing a piece of furniture in the workroom, but he came to the front in time to see the children as they were leaving. He couldn't help but notice how the children were fascinated with the mirror; they again stopped and stared at it before going out the door.

"Do you think they are the ones?" he asked Pearl, after the children were gone.

"I don't know," said Pearl. "But I do hope they will come back. I would like to become better acquainted with them."

One afternoon, Pearl was dusting the items on a shelf and singing to herself, when the bell on the door jingled. She turned around to see the brother and sister come in. After a somewhat shy response to Pearl's greeting, the pair went to stand and stare at the mirror.

"What is it about the mirror that attracts you to it?" Pearl asked the children.

The boy turned and answered hesitantly: "I thought I saw something besides my face in it, when we came last time. I had to come back to see if it would be there again."

"What did you see?" Pearl asked.

"I don't know....it happened so fast," said the boy.

"Did you see something too?" Pearl asked the girl.

"Yes, ma'am, but not for long," answered the girl. "I don't know what it was, but it had many colors."

"Did you see it this time?" Pearl wanted to know.

"No, ma'am," said the boy. "Please don't tell anyone about this---they may think we are crazy."

"I don't think you are crazy," Pearl assured them. "And if you do see something else, please tell me."

"You don't mind if we come back every now and then and check?" asked the boy.

"I don't mind at all," said Pearl. "And I would like to get better acquainted with both of you. Come back anytime."

Several days passed without incident, and Pearl began to wonder if they would ever come.

Suddenly, there they were again. They quietly stepped in and came to stand in front of the mirror. Pearl was glad there were no other customers in the store at the time.

"I saw it! There it is!" exclaimed the girl. "There are lots of flowers!"

"It's a garden," said the boy. "Come look!"

Pearl moved quickly---but not quickly enough. The vision in the mirror had disappeared.

"It's gone," said the girl sadly. "What does it mean?"

"Tell us," said the boy. "Is this mirror magical?"

"No," said Pearl. "But I do believe that you saw something in it that normally could not be seen."

"Then it must be magic!" said the girl.

"What else could it be?" asked the boy.

Rusty walked into the room just at that moment. He had been listening to this strange conversation, although it did not seem strange to him. It was as if a light had been turned on for him, and he suddenly knew what was happening.

"You are some very special children, and you have been given a glimpse into another world," he told the boy and girl.

"What kind of world?" the boy asked suspiciously.

"A very good one," answered Rusty. "At least the part you have seen is a very good place."

"Have you been there?" asked the girl in wide-eyed wonder.

"I came from there," said Rusty. "I think that since you have been allowed to see this world, you have been given the gift to go and visit that world."

"Are you from there too?" the girl asked Pearl.

"Yes, I am," said Pearl, "And it is a beautiful place, filled with flowers like you saw."

"Is it dangerous there?" the child asked.

"There is some danger," answered Pearl. "But there is also someone who will protect you."

"I don't know about all this," said the boy. "This is really weird. Come on, let's go home."

"Roger, I want to find out more about this," protested the girl.

"No," said the boy firmly. "We have to leave." And he grabbed the girl's arm and pulled her towards the door and opened it.

The girl tried to pull free, but her brother wouldn't let go of her arm until they were both outside the shop again. Rusty and Pearl could hear them arguing as they walked away.

Rusty consoled Pearl about the disappointment over the children's reaction. "They're just scared," he said. "I think they will be back. In fact, I'm sure they will be back."

Chapter 3

Rusty was right; the children arrived at the shop again one afternoon. Something was definitely happening; Pearl could sense it now as Rusty had during the children's last visit.

This time, Pearl felt the children's need more strongly than before. She took the initiative to ask the children if they were hungry.

"Yes!" said the girl, although her brother immediately frowned at her and shook his head in a signal for her to keep quiet.

Rusty came in from outside just then and greeted the children warmly, then busied himself at the register, although he was listening carefully. Pearl asked the girl if she would like a peanut butter and jelly sandwich, and saw the response in her eyes that showed she did. So Rusty stayed up front, and Pearl convinced the children to go with her to the little kitchen room, where she made sandwiches for them.

"So how is your mother doing? Did she like the earrings?" asked Pearl, to set them at ease, after handing them each a plate with a sandwich, and a bottle of juice.

Between bites, the girl said that their mother liked the earrings a lot, but she had been sick. That bit of information caused the boy to frown again at his sister. Evidently he was reluctant to share any details about their lives.

Pearl tried to find out more without intruding on their privacy. The girl's name was Sundae, and she was in third grade, and her brother Roger was in seventh grade. Pearl asked about their favorite subjects in school; Sundae liked reading and Roger liked science.

When they had eaten the last bite, Roger stood up and thanked Pearl and told his sister that they needed to leave now. His sister reluctantly stood as well, and she and her brother began walking back to the front, followed by Pearl.

This time, Roger tried to pass by the mirror without looking, but Sundae cried out that she saw it again. So Roger stopped and looked and this time Pearl saw it, too.

They all saw a beautiful garden in the mirror instead of their own reflections. The vision lasted about a minute and then it was gone.

Sundae exclaimed that she would love to go see that garden, but her brother's expression showed apprehension. "Why couldn't we just go and see it?" the girl pleaded with her brother. "They said it isn't magic," she reminded him.

"Then what is it?" asked the boy. "I have to take care of you, Sundae. We can't go to strange places that we know nothing about."

"But *they* know that place," said the girl. "And now we know *them*."

"Not really," said the boy. Then he turned to Pearl and said, "But I do appreciate the food, ma'am."

"You are welcome," answered Pearl. "And I hope you will come back so that we can know each other better."

Pearl saw a little bit of a smile come to the boy's face, but it vanished quickly. He took his sister's arm and drew her to the door, and then they left together. Just as they walked out, Sundae looked back and smiled at Pearl.

Pearl went to the register where Rusty was standing, leaned against him, and sighed. Rusty put his arms around her and said reassuringly, "Sometimes it takes a little while for trust to grow. Their hearts are like a garden---we'll keep watering and waiting."

"The next time they come," said Pearl, "I think I'll plant a seed of promise."

"Yes....I think you should," said Rusty seriously, still holding Pearl in his arms. Then that mischievous smile appeared and he said in a teasing way, "I seem to remember a girl who also took a lot of coaxing to believe what I said."

"Oh, really..." said Pearl and she grinned. "I think I know that girl. She fell in love with some boy with curly red hair who had a habit of talking to birds!" Pearl laughed, then Rusty started laughing, and then they both laughed until they were breathless.

"Rusty..." said Pearl, when she could stop laughing, "Thank you for not giving up on me."

"If I had, I would have missed one of the greatest rewards of my life," said Rusty, with a far-away look in his eyes, as he held Pearl close to himself. "It was all part of a magnificent plan for our lives. And we won't give up on those children, either."

Pearl was ready for the next time the children came; she had written down a particular promise on a note card to give them. Despite the boy's trepidation, the children seemed drawn to the little antique store as if it were a magnet.

This afternoon the boy seemed even more distraught than before. He was very nervous and kept clearing his throat. Sundae seemed tired and listless, and Pearl wondered what was happening in their young lives to cause this. She invited them to have some cookies and milk in the back room. This time, the boy seemed more readily agreeable to go with Pearl to the kitchen room.

After serving them the refreshments, Pearl took the chance to ask what was wrong. She hoped it was not too soon to expect the boy to confide in her. "Are you in some kind of trouble?" Pearl asked.

"No....well, yes," the boy answered. "I haven't been able to talk to anyone about this."

"We are hiding from our father," said the boy and then he looked down as if embarrassed and ashamed.

"Hiding?" Pearl asked, hoping for clarification.

"We move around a lot, so he won't find us. He wants to take us from our mother," said Roger. "Our mother has custody of us, but she's afraid that he will try to get us back."

"She thinks he'll steal us," said Sundae.

"Anyway," said Roger. "Our mother is worried that he may have found us."

"Do you think he is here?" asked Pearl.

Roger shook his head. "I don't know. I didn't want to take the chance, so we didn't go home after school. We came here instead."

"So you have been keeping your sister safe all this time," remarked Pearl. "Now I understand why you didn't talk about yourselves."

"Yes, ma'am," assented Roger. "Our mother has to work a lot to pay the bills and she isn't home very much, so I look after my sister."

"I wrote something down for you, Roger," said Pearl. "This may not make sense to you right now, but in time, I think it will." She handed him the note card on which was written these words: "I will always be there for you; you can depend on me forever."

Roger read it and looked up, very puzzled. "Who is saying this?" he asked.

"Someone who loves you very much, and wants to be like a father to you," said Pearl.

"I'm tired," said Sundae and she put her head down. "I want to go home."

"We can't right now," said Roger. "I don't know if it's safe yet."

"Can we go see that garden in the mirror?" asked Sundae. "Just for a little while?"

"How do we get there?" Roger asked Pearl. "And how do we get back?"

"You mean we can go?" said Sundae, becoming excited.

"I think for you, the way will be through the mirror," said Pearl. "Someone there will show you the way back. Are you still afraid, Roger?"

"Yes, maybe some….but I have been thinking about what we saw….and I wonder why we keep seeing this," said Roger. "I figure the only way to find out would be to go there."

"You are right," answered Pearl. "It may seem risky----but then, most adventures do."

Chapter 4

Pearl and the two children walked back to the front of the store and met up with Rusty. He instinctively knew what was about to take place.

"So you are ready for an adventure?" he asked the children.

"I think so," answered Roger, and Sundae nodded and smiled her agreement.

And so the two children stood by the mirror and looked earnestly in it; and there again was the vision of the lovely garden. Pearl found a stool so that Sundae could reach the mirror and touch it, for Pearl was certain that touch would be required to enter that world. (She remembered this from Audrey's adventure so many years ago.)

Rusty made sure that the bamboo shade in the front store window was down so that no one outside would see this strange event that they knew was about to happen.

And then the children held each other's hands, took a deep breath, and then simultaneously placed their other hand upon the mirror----and in that instant, they were gone.

The next instant, Roger and Sundae found themselves in a very large, very beautiful garden that was more like a manicured forest because of the tall trees dispersed throughout it.

Roger's eyes could barely take it all in, it was so incredibly beautiful; the rich dark blues and reds in the tree bark, and the brilliant green and orange leaves in the treetops made it so startling in color that he felt as if he had stepped into an impressionist's painting.

There was a cool breeze, and it seemed as if it was whispering to him, "Peace." He looked at Sundae and the joy in her eyes was sparkling in the rays of sunshine coming through the tall trees. She was absolutely mesmerized by the scene all around her.

"Roger," she said in an awed hushed voice. "This is better than anything I ever dreamed!"

"It's better than anything I ever dreamed, that's for sure," said Roger, rather dryly. He looked up and saw the strangest thing; instead of moss draping these trees, there was a golden lacy stuff that shimmered in the sunlight.

"Look at that gold stuff in the trees!" said Sundae, looking up and all around. Then she knelt down by some flowers and burst out laughing. "These flowers are giggling when the bees touch the petals!" she exclaimed.

"I didn't hear that," said Roger, somewhat perplexed.

"Maybe you're not listening," said Sundae. "Bend down."

"That's okay," said Roger. "I'm fine with not hearing it."

"Well, you shouldn't be," said Sundae. "There's no reason not to enjoy it."

Roger shrugged, and put his hands in his pockets.

They wandered around the garden paths, and Sundae admired the colors of the bark and touched the trees trunks in wonder. "Did you ever see trees like this before?" she asked her brother.

"No," said Roger. "They probably only exist here in this strange place."

Sundae noticed the many colorful butterflies just then, flitting over the flower blossoms. "Look at how large those butterflies are!" she exclaimed. She began to follow the butterflies around the curving walkways among the clusters of flowers, clapping her hands with delight at everything she saw around her.

"Look at that! There's a well," said Sundae and she ran over to investigate. "And look, here's a dipper to take a drink."

"Don't drink that," warned her brother as he walked closer to the well. "It might be enchanted."

"Welcome," said a voice, and the children turned to see a woman standing in the pathway. She was wearing a long light blue dress and her eyes looked like blue jewels. "The water is perfectly safe for you to drink," she said.

"Oh, good, I'm thirsty," said Sundae, and she drew out some water with the dipper.

"Stop," said Roger. "This woman is a stranger. We don't know if we can believe her."

"Well, I do," said Sundae, and she took a sip before Roger could get to her and stop her. "Mmmm…Roger, this water tastes so good! You have to try it."

Roger hesitantly took a sip, and his expression revealed his surprise at the taste of the water. "That is very unusual water," he remarked.

"Yes, it is," said the woman in the blue dress. "It has been flavored with the Prince's grace and mercy."

Roger looked upset. "I told you we shouldn't drink any!" he told Sundae. "It's enchanted."

"No," said the woman, smiling at them. "It has no enchantment....but everything here in this garden belongs to the Prince and it is very good. This is the Kingdom of Grace."

"Who is this prince?" said Roger.

"He is the son of the King," answered the woman in the blue dress.

"What is this king's name, and what is the name of his son?" Roger wanted to know.

"The king's name is Majesty, and his son's name is Victory---and I am Saphire," she told him. "We have been waiting for you to come."

"How do they know me?" Roger asked, somewhat suspiciously.

"The king and his son can see into your world," was Saphire's reply.

"Do they look through that mirror?" Sundae innocently asked.

"No," said Saphire, and she smiled. "They don't need a mirror to see all that is going on. The mirror was sent to the little antique shop to get your attention."

"Do you know Mr. Rusty and his wife Pearl?" asked Sundae hopefully.

"Yes!" said Saphire joyfully. "I know them very well."

"Why didn't you say that in the first place?" said Roger, in a slightly disgruntled way.

"Roger," said Saphire in a more serious tone of voice, "You have been brought here for your good, not to harm you. Come now, follow me."

Saphire began to walk down the path through the tall trees and Sundae followed her without any hesitation, but Roger ambled along more slowly behind them, as if he was not too sure that he should be doing this.

Sundae could not help expressing her admiration at all the varied colors as they passed through the many rows of flowers on either side of the walkways, and Saphire looked appreciatively at Sundae's exuberance.

"And how do you like it, Roger?" asked Saphire of him, waiting for his response.

"It's a very nice garden," he replied, trying to be a little more enthusiastic.

"The beauty is for you to enjoy," said Saphire, "So the Prince is well pleased when people truly enjoy the splendor, as Sundae is doing." Then turning to Sundae, she said, "You make him happy with your excitement over his garden."

"Where are we going?" asked Sundae, as they came out of the forest garden into a clearing. Here the sky was blue and bright with several clean white puffs of clouds softening the blue.

"I don't want to ruin the wonder of your first look at this place," said Saphire. "Just enjoy the journey along the way, and then you will be surprised when you see your destination up ahead."

"Okay," said Sundae with satisfaction at this answer, for she did enjoy nice surprises---which in her young life, had happened only rarely.

CHAPTER 5

The trio proceeded through the clearing and came to a little wooden bridge with low walls running the length of it. It passed over a swiftly moving brook and as they came to the middle of the bridge, Sundae heard flute-like music coming from below her feet.

"How peculiar this place is!" she cried. "The brook is making music like flutes!" And she stopped and stood still on the bridge to listen. And then she saw something stranger still; she saw a group of animals who came to the clearing and began to dance to the music.

"Have these animals been trained in a circus of some sort?" Sundae asked in bewilderment.

"No," said Saphire, who was their guide. "All of creation here is praising the Prince for his grace and love for all of his creatures. When they hear the music of the brook, they spontaneously dance, in honor of the Prince."

"Oh…this is a very remarkable place," said Sundae with reverence in her voice. Saphire smiled in genuine delight over this realization by the young girl.

I am sad to say that Roger did not feel the elation that Sundae expressed. Yet Saphire did not reprove him or scold him in the least, for she knew more about him than she admitted.

They continued on their journey, passing by golden fields of something that looked like wheat stalks, waving in the wind. The wind was cool, but the sun was warm on their backs. Behind them in the distance there was a blue and purple mountain peak, as they turned and continued to walk alongside the brook under trees growing on either side of it.

The children heard a sound much like wind chimes and they were very puzzled by this, until they realized that the sound was made by the leaves on the trees. It was a beautiful ethereal sound, and they walked along without speaking as they listened in wonder. Even Roger was in awe at this unusual aspect of the woods by the brook.

As they walked, they caught glimpses of something white glistening through the trees. Eventually, their path turned away from the brook and the woods and they stepped out into a field of brilliant purple and white flowers with blue and pink ones beyond these. And now they could clearly see the glistening white object ahead; it was a white castle set high up on a hill.

"Is that where we are going?" inquired Sundae with jubilation, as they stopped to gaze at this sight.

"Yes," said Saphire. "That is indeed where we are going. That, my young friend, is the palace of the Prince."

And suddenly, another person came out of the woods into the meadow of flowers. His hair was long and wavy, and he was wearing the rough clothing of a peasant farmer of long ago.

He wore brown trousers, a long tunic with billowy sleeves, brown boots, a brown sash, and he carried a staff. He also had a shoulder satchel with the strap worn diagonally across his chest. But the most distinctive thing about this person was his eyes; they were such a deep aquamarine blue that Roger felt as if he was looking into the ocean when he saw those eyes.

"Greetings," said the man with a large smile as he joined the group on the path.

Roger was startled by the man's sudden appearance and equally uncomfortable with the man's company, especially as this stranger seemed intent on walking with them. Roger instinctively tried to move between the stranger and his sister.

"I mean no harm to either you or your sister," said the man who had joined them.

"Does everyone here know who we are?" Roger asked with some misgivings.

The man smiled, and then he answered: "Your identity is safe with Saphire and with me. Yes, I do know who you are, Roger and Sundae Cobban."

And then there was no time to protest this invasion of privacy, for they were coming to the tall blue spruce trees which bordered the castle grounds. They passed through the border of trees, beyond which were small farms and a village, and kept on until they came to the stone walkway leading up to the castle entrance. Sundae was so excited that she felt she might forget to breathe, and Roger felt his duty keenly to protect his sister in this strange place, although he had no confidence of his ability to do so. And so there was a great contrast and tension felt between Sundae's eagerness, and Roger's apprehension.

Sundae could not be dissuaded from her anticipation, even by her brother's reluctance, and she began jumping from one colored diagonal stone to the next, hardly waiting for her guide. Saphire did not mind Sundae's reckless enthusiasm; she laughed to see it. But tension was mounting in Roger; he wanted at least to encourage more caution in his sister, but she refused any part of it.

Next, they came to a series of brick steps leading up to the gateway and corridor of the castle entryway. Sundae stopped here and waited for Saphire to accompany her up these steps, and Roger was glad of that.

But when they arrived at the steps, Saphire had a shocking announcement. She said, "Sundae and I will go on from here. Roger, you are not yet ready to meet with the Prince, and you must stay with the Shepherd until you are prepared."

"What did I do to you to deserve this!" yelled Roger in anger. "You have no right!"

"A person cannot enter unless they humble themselves in the same manner as a little child," said Saphire gently.

"No!" protested Roger. "You cannot separate us--- it is my job to take care of my sister! I won't let you do this!" and he made a vain attempt to pull his sister away from Saphire.

A strong arm restrained him; the Shepherd's great strength surprised him and he could not prevail against it. "Roger," said the Shepherd kindly. "You are carrying a weight that is too heavy for you, and you are weary. You have come here so that I can give you rest."

And suddenly Roger broke down and cried, for he was very, very weary---and when the Shepherd put his arms around him in an embrace, Roger didn't resist at all. He laid his head on the Shepherd's chest and sobbed.

Sundae was torn between her concern for her brother and her desire to go in the Palace, but Roger finally got his sobs under control enough to give his sister his consent for her to go. Sundae looked up at Saphire for affirmation, and Saphire nodded. "Your brother will be in good hands," she told Sundae, "And he will join you just as soon as possible."

The Shepherd and Roger stood watching together as Saphire escorted Sundae up the brick steps, through the black wrought-iron gate, and on into the stone corridor leading to the castle door. Sundae stopped and looked at the words above the door; she seemed uncertain, but whatever Saphire told her at that moment appeared to satisfy her. Sundae turned and waved, and then they went in.

Roger let out a big sigh, as if releasing all the pent-up tension he had been feeling for so long.

"Come with me," said the Shepherd, "And I will show you where I live."

"Is it far from here?" Roger asked.

"Do you see that mountain in the distance?" asked the shepherd.

"Yes..." Roger replied.

"My cottage is at the base of that mountain. Come, let's go there now," said the Shepherd.

They were walking down the stone walkway again, following the path through the small farms and the village, when Roger was reminded of his mother and he felt a pang of guilt.

"You are worried about your mother," said the Shepherd. "Time is different here; it will not even seem as if you are gone, though much may take place here."

"How did you know what I was thinking?" asked Roger.

The Shepherd merely smiled and kept walking. "Come," he said. "I have so much to teach you so that you will be ready to join your sister."

They went back through the meadow of flowers and back through the woods by the brook, and here they found fruit growing that looked to Roger like small pink bananas. He found they tasted like strawberry and banana, and he liked them very much. They continued on their way, turning onto a different path that led closer to the mountain. It was late afternoon by now and the sun was a descending ball of orange fire with streaks of lavender around it. Still, its golden rays illumined the brilliant greens in the grasses and the blue and pink wildflowers, though shining lower near the ground. There was a large flat rock close by, and the Shepherd proposed that they sit there and have some refreshment. By this, he meant some sweet and nutty bread which he shared with Roger, and some water from a canteen.

There was a cool breeze which tickled Roger's hair, but the sun still warmed his back. He looked around and reveled in the landscape; this was something he had been unable to do for some time, as his mind had been too preoccupied with the pressure of hiding.

The Shepherd said nothing, for this moment required nothing. Roger sat near him and was not uncomfortable with this silence. He felt more at ease than ever he could remember. When he looked up and saw a large dark object in the distance, he was more grieved at being disturbed than he was afraid.

But as this dark object came closer and closer, Roger began to be alarmed. The object came into focus, and Roger observed in horror that it was a huge bird with gigantic talons. It began to circle around them and to scream with a shrill piercing cry.

Roger tried to speak calmly, but his voice had a tremor as he asked the Shepherd about this bird. "It is a bird of prey," said the Shepherd, without showing any sign of dread or fear. "What does it hunt?" asked the boy in his now shaky voice. The Shepherd's reply made him shudder, for his answer was that this thing preyed on children. Yet Roger was comforted in some small way, for he detected a fierce anger in the Shepherd's voice.

"This creature is not from the kingdom of Grace," said the Shepherd. "It comes from the kingdom of shadows, there by the gray mountain," and he pointed it out to the boy. "Do not let it make you afraid, for that is what it is trying to do. I am with you and it cannot harm you."

As the bird flew lower and lower and its shrill cry tortured his ears, Roger watched as the Shepherd took a leather slingshot from his bag and a sharp stone. With the strength of a javelin thrower, the Shepherd whirled the sling. The rock flew out with such velocity, and struck the bird with such force, that it shrieked with agony, turned sharply and flew away to its lair on the gray mountain.

Then the Shepherd stood, and said, "Come, let us be going," and he began to walk along the path toward the blue and purple mountain. And as they went the Shepherd began to sing, and these were the words of his song: "I have loved you from the dawn of time, long before the world began; I have known you in your mother's womb---I have called you by your name."

They were much closer now to the base of the mountain, and there Roger saw a small stone cottage and he was very relieved, for it was almost night time now. The Shepherd greeted a fellow shepherd who had brought the flock of sheep into the fold for the night. Roger and the Shepherd entered the cottage; and Roger was so tired that when the Shepherd showed him his place to sleep up in the loft, he went immediately and fell into a deep sleep.

Chapter 6

When Roger woke up the next morning, he forgot where he was, and had a moment of panic and confusion. Then he looked around; sunshine was streaming in over him from a small window in the loft, and he put his hands out and felt straw around him. It had a crispy feeling under the soft flannel blankets he was lying on. The pillow he was using smelled like honeysuckles---at least, that was the closest description he could compare it to in his mind. There was silence except for the birds singing outside. That was different; there were no street sounds of cars passing by, or sirens of ambulances, or large trucks braking.

He climbed down from the loft and looked for the Shepherd, but he was not there. But on the table, there was food set out---for him, he presumed. There was juice in a large cup and some type of bread on a plate, and another plate had fruit of some kind that he had never seen before. He discovered that he was very hungry, and the food here tasted very good. The shepherd's cottage was primitive, he observed, and there was no sink. So he took his dishes outside and saw a washing area by the well. Washing dishes outside was a novel thing for him, as he had never been camping. He dried them and put them back in the cupboard against the wall by the table inside.

He set out to look for the Shepherd, who he saw was up on the side of the mountain, but not too high for a novice like himself to go and meet him. So he did, clambering over rocks and brush and small crevices. "Hello," he said when he was within hearing range of the Shepherd. "Good morning!" called the Shepherd. "Did you sleep well?"

Roger was close enough now to hold a conversation, and he answered, "Yes, I did." "So you had no nightmares?" said the Shepherd, looking at Roger intently.

"No, sir, I didn't," Roger replied. "You knew I have nightmares?"

"Yes," said the Shepherd. "You often dream of people stealing your sister, and you are helpless to save her, and then you wake up tormented."

Roger looked at him incredulously, wondering how he knew these things.

"I told you that I brought you here to give you rest," said the Shepherd, "And that is what I intend to do."

"What will be required of me?" asked Roger, for he assumed there would be a price for this benefit.

"In the Kingdom of Grace these things are free," said the Shepherd. "All that I ask is that you listen to me, and follow my instructions."

"Okay, fair enough," said Roger.

Roger spent that day up on the mountainside with the Shepherd, learning about the ways of sheep and how to care for them.

"They will only follow me because they know my voice," said the Shepherd. "Here, I'll show you what I mean. Do you see that large bush over there?" he said, indicating a shrub in another area. "This fellow is named Sydney. Go to that bush and then call him."

Roger complied, and did as he asked, but the sheep known as Sydney merely stared at the one calling him, and stayed exactly where he was.

"Come back," called the Shepherd, and Roger walked back over to him. "Now watch," the Shepherd told Roger, as he walked the distance over to the bush.

As soon as he called Sydney, the sheep obediently went to him. In fact, the whole flock of sheep started to move in that direction, until the Shepherd began to walk back with Sydney.

"Sydney was a bummer lamb," explained the Shepherd. "The ewe---the mother---rejected him as a baby lamb, and I had to care for him myself at my cottage. He was always close to me, so he trusts me completely, and now he is a bellwether sheep---a leader of the flock."

They had cheese and bread and fruit for lunch, and water from a canteen that didn't taste at all like water from home---or any other place that he had lived. He couldn't describe it—(and neither can I) but for a person who normally did not like water, he would say it was wonderful.

When the Shepherd wanted the sheep to lie down and rest, he brought out a flute from his bag and began to play a song in a minor key. It was a haunting melody, but so relaxing that Roger fell asleep, too, lying on the grass.

He woke up in a little while, because something was tickling his nose. It was one of those very large butterflies; it had landed on his nose and seemed to be staring at him. His eyes crossed as he looked at it, and the Shepherd burst out laughing. Yet he didn't sense any ridicule in the laughter; there was a different feeling about it altogether. That puzzled him; he had not experienced many adult relationships that did not have ridicule as an element.

"Come," said the smiling Shepherd, as he reached out his strong arm to lift Roger to his feet. "We must bring the sheep to get water." He led the way with Sydney, and the other sheep following, to a trickling brook in a ravine of the mountain. The sheep seemed to take turns stepping down into the water and drinking, then climbing out for the next group.

Roger caught a glimpse of a shadow of something, moving stealthily behind rocks and shrubs. In a moment he realized the danger; the shadow was moving toward the more defenseless young sheep in the flock. He saw it spring upon the lamb so swiftly that the lamb had no time to run; but the shepherd was upon it in an instant and beat it off with a club. Roger guessed it was a mountain lion---a cougar--- though he had only seen this animal before in picture books. The wild cat whimpered in pain and slunk away into the growing shadows on the mountain.

Then the Shepherd examined the lamb; it was only slightly wounded, and he poured oil from a flask into the wound, picked up the lamb and put it on his shoulders.

When the other sheep had finished drinking, the Shepherd told Roger that it was time to take them home. So they slowly made their way down the mountainside, checking for any who were straying from the path, and guiding them back with a staff. The Shepherd assigned this task to Roger, after showing him how to use the staff.

It was late afternoon when they arrived at the cottage, and the Shepherd guided the sheep into the fold and closed the gate. After checking the hurt lamb's wounds and applying more ointment, the Shepherd released it into the fold to join the others.

While the Shepherd and Roger were having their supper at the rough wooden table in the cottage, Roger realized he had not thought much about his sister that day, and he felt a twinge of guilt. Then the Shepherd said, "Tomorrow we will go and see your sister."

It seemed to Roger that the Shepherd possessed an uncanny ability to know what he was thinking, and that it had to be more than coincidence. Yet he was beginning to feel a security from this novelty rather than an intrusion. He rather doubted that he would have known how to express his thoughts in any cohesive fashion anyway---and here was someone who understood his incoherent and mixed-up thoughts perfectly.

He lay on his straw bed covered with soft blankets, looking up at the stars through the loft window, and thought about the things the Shepherd had told him. He had said, "Roger, you have gifts locked up inside you. You are not who your father said you are; he is speaking out of his own disappointment and pain about himself."

Roger had asked the Shepherd, "Do you know my father too?" And the answer was affirmative, leaving more questions in Roger's mind.

Roger asked about the unlocking of these gifts, whatever they were; how would that take place? The shepherd told him he would find out when he met the Prince----that there he would discover the ancient secret.

Everything about this place was mysterious, and one mystery only led to another. Perhaps this ancient secret would unravel them all, Roger thought. But he would not be able to find it out unless he was prepared enough to meet the Prince; and how would that preparation be accomplished? He wondered if he was any closer to that goal, though it seemed a paradox. How could one progress to a goal without any concept of the goal itself?

But the stars were speaking to him---twinkling and winking at him in a dark blue velvet sky, suspended over the mountain, the grass, the trees, the flowers---as if they were saying, "Be still. There is glory here and you will find the answer."

And he slept deeply through the night.

Chapter 7

Roger woke up early; the birds were singing and the sunlight was spilling over him from the loft window. It felt like peace was pouring over him in that little loft room. He just lay there for a moment, enjoying this feeling. There was no sound from below, so he assumed the Shepherd was not there. He threw off the blankets and climbed down the ladder, and there was breakfast laid out on the table for him. He sat down and gratefully ate what the Shepherd had provided for him. Though the food here was simple, it was very nourishing.

In just a moment, the Shepherd entered and greeted him. "Today, we will go and see your sister," he told the boy seated at his table.

"Thank you for the breakfast," Roger said. "You are very welcome," said the Shepherd. "I am happy to have your company."

The Shepherd showed Roger where he could wash up, and gave him a set of clean clothes. They were similar in fashion to that of the Shepherd's clothing, and yet they were Roger's own size. "Where did you find these?" he asked curiously. "From a young man in the village who is about your age," said the Shepherd. "He didn't mind loaning some of his clothes for a friend."

"But I don't even know him," protested Roger. "I will introduce you," was the Shepherd's reply, "And you will find in him a friend."

After Roger washed up and changed his clothes, the Shepherd and he set out to go to the castle. A shepherd from the village had already taken the flock of sheep up to the mountainside to graze, so there was no need of that.

So the Shepherd and the boy walked along the path from the cottage through the meadow and away from the mountain. Roger again felt that peace as they walked in the sunshine; he felt it also in the shade under the trees by the brook. Maybe peace isn't a place, he thought to himself; maybe it is found wherever the Shepherd is. He looked up at the Shepherd, and their eyes met and the Shepherd smiled at him.

"You will find that your sister is changed," said the Shepherd. This somewhat troubled Roger, as he felt responsible for his sister, and he had not been there to make sure this change was a good one. "Do not fret," said the Shepherd. "It is a very good change, and she is happy."

"When will I be ready to meet the Prince?" asked Roger. "That depends on you," said the Shepherd. Roger sighed at that answer; it still did nothing to give him any clue as to how to prepare himself. "Do I have to prepare myself or what?" he asked. "No," said the Shepherd, as they turned away from the brook and towards the tree border of the castle grounds.

"Your responses to situations are what will indicate your readiness," said the Shepherd.

Roger frowned to himself; he still didn't understand what the Shepherd meant, but he didn't want to keep asking and get more of the same ambiguous answers, so he said nothing.

They had now come to the colorful stone walkway leading to the brick steps which went up to the castle corridor and entryway. Roger could see that there were people waiting in that corridor, and his sister was among them.

There were also tables covered with white cloths on the lawn around the castle, and servers were bringing platters of food out to these. Roger realized it was past lunchtime, and he was hungry, so he was excited to see this particular activity.

The Shepherd indicated that Roger could go on and meet his sister, and he would meet up with him later. "Then you're not coming?" asked Roger in surprise. "I will not be far from you," said the Shepherd. "I will not abandon you, so go---enjoy your time with your sister."

The Shepherd turned and went back the way they had come. He turned and waved to Roger, who had not moved. Finally, Roger walked closer to the castle and as he did, Sundae came running towards him and hugged him very tightly.

"Roger!" she exclaimed, "I have missed you!" She took his hand and drew him to the area with the tables. There were other people sitting around the tables now, and Saphire approached Roger and his sister and invited them to sit at one of these tables. People were still bringing platters of food from the castle kitchen, but when that was finished, a young man stood and blessed the food and then the people began to eat.

"That is Cedric," said Sundae, indicating the young man who had blessed the food. "He's friends with Mr. Rusty and Pearl."

Roger looked at this man curiously; he wondered what kind of childhood these people had experienced here. Surely it had been much different than his childhood. And then he looked at Sundae; there was definitely something different about her---what was it? Was it some kind of radiance showing in her face?

"What happened to you here?" he asked after he had eaten several sandwiches and washed them down with lemonade.

"A lot!" said Sundae excitedly. "I met the Prince, and he is wonderful! I have never met anyone like him before. I can't wait until you get to meet him, too! And look at my dress! They made this just for me. And do you know what? The Prince adopted me."

"Sundae, we already have parents," Roger said suspiciously. "You don't need anyone to adopt you. And we are not staying here, remember?"

"Roger, it's not like that. He adopted me as one of his children in his kingdom," she explained. "He knows I still have a mother and a father---even if my father is sick."

"He isn't sick----he's crazy," said Roger with contempt.

"And you know what?" said Sundae. "We are all sick with a disease called sin. The only way to be healed is to let the Prince put his antidote inside your heart."

"How does he do that?" asked Roger, even more suspiciously than before.

"With his scepter," said Sundae. "There's a ceremony and everything."

"That sounds weird, Sundae," said Roger. "I need to get you away from here."

"It isn't weird," said Sundae. "It's the most beautiful thing that has ever happened to me. I have never been this happy before. The Prince loves us, Roger----it's his love that makes me so happy. Even if you take me away from here, that love is going to stay in my heart because he said 'I will always be there for you; you can depend on me forever.'"

Roger frowned and then he said, "This story just sounds too good to be true."

"But why do true things have to be bad things?" Sundae asked. "It seems to me that if something is true, then it would be good, because truth is good, not bad."

"Truth isn't always good," said Roger.

"Yes, it is," argued Sundae. "It is lies that are bad."

"I don't know if I can believe in this," said Roger, "even if something did happen here."

"I am telling you the truth!" Sundae asserted. "And I sure hope you get to see for yourself."

"Fine, Sundae," said Roger angrily. "Just believe what you want, but don't expect me to. I don't think they were fair anyway----why did you get to go in and I didn't? Do you think that was fair?"

"Roger, I don't know why I got to go in first...," began Sundae, but Roger cut her off.

"I'll tell you why. It's because they think you are so special, but I'm not. I've spent all this time trying to protect you, but that wasn't enough to get me in to the castle! No, they picked you over me---they thought you deserved the special treatment, but I wasn't worth it!" Roger was so angry and upset that he got up and walked away.

"Don't leave!" Sundae cried out after him. "It's not like that!"

But Roger ignored her pleas and kept walking away. Saphire walked over to Sundae and comforted her. Roger looked back and saw this, and it made him even angrier. She gets all the attention, he said to himself. She is the privileged one; even after all I have done to take care of her, I am left out----and they don't even care!

Roger was so angry that he kept on walking until he was back in the original garden where he and Sundae had first arrived, and it was here that he met another man---who was very different.

Chapter 8

This man was dressed in black clothing, and his hair was thick and black and perfectly arranged. His eyes were black and yellow, and he was carrying a large mirror.

"Hello," said the man. "You look as if something very disagreeable has happened."

"Yes," said Roger. "It did."

"That's a shame," said the man. "But of course that is to be expected when people don't want to face reality. In this place, the people prefer to believe in a fairy tale."

"What do you know about this?" asked Roger, not wanting to be gullible.

"Oh, everything you need to know….that they have kept from you," said the man. "They cheat you and then reprimand you for being resentful. They are not fair or trustworthy."

Roger was beginning to think that possibly this man was telling the truth, and that his sister had been very deceived. If that were so, then perhaps this man would be the one who could help him get her out of the castle and away from here.

"What is that mirror you're holding?" he asked.

"Oh...I'm glad you asked. This is a portal to take you to a place where you will find the knowledge you seek, and the reality that you need," said the man. "If you remain here, they will only make you look foolish-----but I will make you wiser than they are."

"Well...I don't know...I think I need to see some proof of what you are saying," said Roger uncertainly.

"Oh? And I thought you would see that I was sent here just at the right time to help you," said the man, as he started to walk away. "But I suppose some people are just not ready to face reality," he said as he continued to walk away.

"Wait....," said Roger. "Let me see your mirror."

"Certainly," said the man, and he walked back and held the mirror up so Roger could look in it. Roger saw an elegant castle on a mountainside, and a colorful village in the valley below.

"Is that the place you meant?" he asked the man.

"Yes," answered the man. "I am the king of that region, and I have personally come to escort you away from this place."

"Me?" asked Roger incredulously.

"Yes," said the man. "We have taken a great interest in you, Roger."

Roger was surprised at this, and very flattered. The man went on to say, "We feel you have great potential, even if others have failed to recognize it. Let us help you develop this."

Now Roger was convinced, and he asked the man about the portal; and the man said that he would only need to place his hand upon the mirror, and he would be instantly transported.

Since that was exactly how the other mirror had worked, he had no qualms about this one, so he reached his hand out and touched the mirror.

But he quickly found out that this mirror was NOT like the other one had been; he found himself trapped between the two worlds; he was trapped IN the mirror somehow. He could look out and see around him, but he was held captive by glass walls and could not get out. He was screaming and banging on the glass walls, but the man simply looked at Roger's reflection in the mirror with a very smug, satisfied smile.

Then the man began walking away from the beautiful garden, carrying the mirror with Roger inside it, and headed out into the wilderness beyond the garden and the meadows. Roger wept as they left the garden behind, and painfully watched out of the mirror glass as they went through all the Kingdom of Grace and passed beyond its borders. It was the most dismal journey he had ever been on, and it seemed endless.

The terrain they were in now was desolate and gray, almost as empty as the lifeless moon, Roger thought to himself. There was almost nothing green growing here at all. The wind howled plaintively and eerily and even the sunlight seemed gray and bleak.

They passed through a very dark, dense wood; it was murky and full of strange sounds and even the trees seemed to mumble and threaten and curse at him. This is worse than my nightmares, thought Roger to himself. There was nothing he could do but endure the horror. Then just as they were coming out of the woods, a whole bevy of bats flew in a stream around him. Some of the bats came right up to the mirror, so that suddenly he was staring face to face with a bat and he shrieked in terror.

The man didn't care and he strode on through the wilderness. At last a carriage pulled by horses came to meet them, and the man got in while holding onto the mirror. The rest of the trip was monotonous and very bumpy, and they finally arrived at a very dark gray damp looking castle on the side of a dark gray mountain. It looked nothing like the image the mirror had shown Roger.

He could look down into the valley and see the village, and it was equally as colorless and drab as the castle. The carriage stopped at the beginning of the drawbridge over the moat, and the man got out, still carrying the mirror. The two guards there acknowledged the sovereign ruler with a bow, then stood aside for him to pass between them. Two more guards at the portcullis paid homage to the man and stepped aside to allow him to enter the great door, which was opened by another guard.

Then the man entered the dark castle, and Roger saw a grim and foreboding interior; there were no cheery sights or sounds of any hospitality. The atmosphere was cold and dank, and the wind moaned around all the turrets and corners of the castle walls.

The only light came from some smoky torches in brackets on the walls. The man walked briskly through the castle to the inner courtyard, and again into another wing of the castle. This one apparently was where some of the servants lived;

there was squalor throughout, and the smell of beer, sweat, and urine pervaded the room in which the man now entered.

And it was here that he deposited the mirror, and brought Roger out of it. Roger furtively looked around and saw instruments of torture hanging on the walls of this room. There was a post attached to the floor in the center of the room, and a burly man approached.

"Flog him," said the man in black to the other man, indicating Roger as the subject of this treatment, and the burly man picked up a whip.

"Take yer shirt off," said the burly man and he grinned in a malicious way. "We don't want to mess up yer purty clothes."

"Why are you doing this? I thought you were going to teach me!" cried Roger.

The man in black looked at Roger with a sneer on his face and answered: "This is your first lesson, Roger. You have to learn that I am totally in control here, and you had better do exactly as you are told or there will always be unpleasant consequences."

Then to the burly man, the man in black gave the orders: "Seven lashes will be sufficient," he said and he left the room.

The burly man pulled Roger's shirt off roughly and threw it aside, then bound Roger's hands to the post and made him get down on his knees. Then he proceeded to lash Roger's back with the whip, relishing every crack of the whip as it tore Roger's flesh, and every scream that came from Roger's throat. The man seemed to take his time to make his sadistic pleasure in this beating last longer, as the blood ran trickling down Roger's back onto the floor.

The burly man was about to raise the whip for the eighth lashing, when Roger cried, "He said seven lashes! Can't you count?" The burly man hit Roger on the side of the head with the wooden handle of the whip, and said, "That's for yer sass!"

The burly man untied Roger, handed Roger his shirt, and pushed him in the direction of another doorway. "Go in there," he said. "That's where you'll stay."

The man pushed Roger into the room, slammed the heavy door shut, and locked it from the outside. Roger sat down on the only chair in the room. His head throbbed from the blow of the whip handle and his back was burning as if it was on fire. The pain was excruciating, and he wanted to lie down, but he was concerned about the filth on the floor and his open wounds. He couldn't put his shirt back on for he feared the fabric would stick to the wounds as his blood dried. Where was the Shepherd when he needed him so badly?

If ever there was a time that he regretted something, there was never a time such as this. Tears rolled down his cheeks, and his heart ached as painfully as the wounds on his body.

Now he was a captive to this sinister person because he had listened to his lies.

Chapter 9

Roger did not know the depths of despair until that night, even if he previously thought he had. After some time, someone shoved a plate under the door; it had a piece of moldy bread on it. It was immediately followed by several rats which ran under the door and attacked the bread before he could even examine it.

He finally dared to put his shirt on, and then surveyed this miserable room. There was no place to relieve one's self; there was no toilet, only a bucket in the corner. The stench was terrible, though it would have been far worse, were it not for several narrow openings for windows high in the wall. These had no screens, and allowed several flies to bother him unceasingly, until he decided to smash them with his hands. He had to wipe this on his pants, but as they were already ruined from blood stains, he did not think it would matter so much. He hoped that the unknown friend who had loaned them to him would forgive him.

It was dark outside now; he could observe this from the small windows and he tried to contrive some means of sleeping. He sat on the floor with his legs folded and crossed, and leaned his head and right arm on the seat of the chair.

Just then, he heard a key turn in the door, and the door swung open on rusty hinges. He saw a dark shadowy figure carrying a mirror; the person, whoever it was, set up this mirror on a stand in front of Roger. Then the person left the room, shut the door, and locked it. In the gloom, Roger saw the reflection of the mirror from the little bit of starlight now coming through the windows. "Oh torturous image!" he thought with bitter irony. "The one thing I never wanted to see again, they have put before me," he thought.

And then thoughts began to emanate from the glimmering mirror, as if it were a living thing. The thoughts murmured like a coarse whisper inside his head, and this is what he heard:

"You are here because you are an immense failure. You have no future, for there is nothing in you that is valuable to anyone at all. You are worthless and undesirable. This is reality."

All night long, the whispering went on; the thoughts from this mirror of lies continued. "Look at yourself. You are nothing; you are insignificant and useless. Your life has no effect on anything or anyone. You are inferior and ignorant and unwanted. This is reality."

"You have no capabilities or skills; you are unattractive, dull, awkward and stupid. The only way to survive is to fight; hurt others before they hurt you. This is reality."

"Life is meaningless, and love is only a fairy tale. Your very existence is unnecessary. People are nothing more than animals, so violence is perfectly normal. This is reality."

"Do whatever you feel like doing at the moment, for that is what is natural. Since people are only animals, it does not matter what you do to anyone else. This is reality."

The whispers continued, on and on through the night, without any relief. He could not get away from the barrage of thoughts that infiltrated his mind with such stealth. He tried to think other thoughts, but he had nothing with which to replace these despairing thoughts.

So eventually, he began to accept them. What other truth could there be if this was reality? He would be a fool if he did not accept reality---he would become only a delusional, deluded person "out of touch" with reality.

Roger began to feel as if he were losing his mind, (which he was) and he felt very ill. Then he had a sudden flash of insight; what if this was how his own father felt? For the first time, he began to have a slight feeling of compassion for his own father, who doubtless was mentally disturbed. He remembered that his father had begun to display these mental disorders when he came back from his service in the war.

At the first gleam of morning light, there was a great commotion, and Roger wondered what was happening, but he was in too much of a stupor to investigate or even get up. Then someone unlocked the door, and yanked him up by his arm and dragged him out of the room.

This person pushed him out into the inner courtyard of the castle, and he stood there blinking in the gray light of daybreak. When his eyes adjusted, he saw the legs of a white horse, and as his eyes traveled upward, he saw a magnificent warhorse with a flowing mane and tail, and the man seated on this horse was none other than the Shepherd.

The Shepherd was conversing with someone; Roger's eyes began to focus better and he saw it was the man dressed in black---but he looked different than before. Where was the thick black hair? For now the man was completely bald, and he had bony ridges emerging from the center of the back of his head and more down his neck.

Even in this gray early morning light, Roger could see that his skin color was tinged with green.

"You cannot have him," said the man in black. "He is mine because he came willingly." When he heard this, the fog in Roger's mind lifted enough for him to grasp what was said, and he reacted to this statement. He yelled, "He tricked me!"

The Shepherd looked at Roger, and he said, "Yes, I know. And he will also tell you that I am the one who has deceived you."

"He did," acknowledged Roger. "Do you see now who is speaking truth?" asked the Shepherd. "Yes, it is you," answered Roger, looking down in his shame. The Shepherd implored him, "Come back to me and I will deliver you out of this place."

Then the Shepherd addressed the man in black and he said, "You cannot keep him here." The man in black answered with a mocking tone, "Oh, but I can if he is unwilling to go with you. Even *you* cannot go against his free will."

"Such a shame," said the man in black. "Roger, I thought you would recognize reality. But I can't help you if you insist on following a fantasy."

The Shepherd turned to Roger and said, "Roger, do you want to stay here and serve this person? If you are willing to obey me, I can set you free. You become the servant of whoever you choose to obey."

"He's a tyrant, you fool!" yelled the man in black. "You will become his slave!"

"And what were *you* going to make of me?" Roger retorted in anger. Then Roger came closer to the horse upon which the Shepherd was seated. He looked into the eyes of the Shepherd and earnestly asked, "Do you want me?" In reply, the Shepherd removed his shirt and as the sun was coming up, Roger saw in its light that the Shepherd had seven large deep scars on his upper torso. "I was pierced for you," said the Shepherd. "This is the proof that I want you." He pulled his shirt over himself again, and extended his hand to Roger.

Roger took his hand, and with a firm grasp on Roger's arm, the Shepherd hoisted him onto the back of the horse. With Roger seated behind him, the Shepherd turned the horse around and headed for the castle gate. They passed through the castle itself in a long corridor, then through the portcullis, and on out through the gate. When they were past all of this, the Shepherd advised Roger to hold on, and Roger put his arms around the Shepherd as the horse began to gallop.

The white horse, whose name was Magnificent, went at a hard gallop for some time, her tail and mane lifted by the wind and flowing away from her body as she sped. Roger had never ridden a horse, and he hung on tightly.

When they were well beyond the village, the Shepherd reined her in to a walk. "We're going to give the horse a chance to rest," he told Roger. "You will need to slide off. Put your left foot in the stirrup and bring your right leg over her back."

Roger managed to do this, and then the Shepherd dismounted. They began to walk, with the Shepherd leading the horse by the reins. The Shepherd took out his canteen and gave it to Roger, who was incredibly thirsty by now. He drank and drank; he had never been so grateful for water before this day. Then the Shepherd gave the horse some water in a shallow wooden bowl. They continued walking after the Shepherd put this and the canteen back in the saddle bag, and then the Shepherd began to speak to Roger.

"Did you really choose me----or did you just want to be delivered from your misery?" the Shepherd asked Roger, looking at him intently.

"Does it make any difference?" asked Roger. "Yes," said the Shepherd. "It will make a difference. As long as there is bitterness in you, you are still a captive."

"But what can I do about it?" asked Roger. "I can't help how I feel."

"You hurt your sister," said the Shepherd gently. "And you must deal with that." And then the Shepherd began to tell Roger a story.

Chapter 10

Roger and the Shepherd continued to walk alongside each other through the wilderness as the Shepherd told Roger this story:

"There once were two brothers....one believed, and one resisted. The one who believed understood that in order to be blessed and receive favor, something had to die. He had to let his old self die and be made new. The other brother resisted this; he thought he could reform himself with his own deeds---but he could not. He resented his brother because his brother received the blessing of favor and honor and he didn't---and this resentment grew until he destroyed his own brother. There was someone who would have helped him, but he would not ask because he did not trust or believe in the one who offered his help."

The Shepherd paused, and then he said, "You think the Prince has cheated you---and you don't trust him---and you don't believe your sister."

Roger was petulant, and answered, "But all that stuff the Prince told her! And I don't know if it's true---"

The Shepherd turned abruptly and stopped. He looked at Roger and some kind of fiery light shone out of those deep blue eyes, like a blazing sunset on the water. It shocked Roger and he stood still; he had to look away from the fire in those eyes. The Shepherd spoke with a fierceness Roger had not heard before, and he said: "Let me tell you this: the Prince will never deceive a child! Never! Not with any fairy tales or anything untrue!"

The Shepherd began walking again, and Roger did too, although he was silent for a while. He did not know what to say, but he remembered the anger he had seen in the Shepherd over the birds of prey that accosted children. It seemed to him that the Shepherd must have a fearsome protective instinct towards children, if that is what you could call it, he thought. If only he could trust this Prince as he was learning to trust the Shepherd.

After a little while, the Shepherd said they would ride again, and he mounted Magnificent and reached out his hand to Roger. Roger took hold of his hand, and with a firm grip on his forearm, the Shepherd again lifted Roger into the saddle behind him. They rode without speaking, for the Shepherd's back was to Roger, and he would not be heard. At the Shepherd's command, the horse began to canter, which was a much smoother gait and a more comfortable ride for Roger. When the horse slowed down to a trot now and then, Roger bounced up and down quite a bit, and due to his sleeping position during the night, he was already stiff and sore. They walked some to alleviate the stiffness, and stopped frequently after riding, to give the horse water after her exertions.

This landscape offered nothing refreshing whatsoever; it was barren and gray with dust and afforded little relief from monotony. The dust was the bane of travelers, and the Shepherd fashioned turbans for Roger and he, which shielded their eyes and covered their mouths.

It was worse now so the Shepherd put a sort of hood with blinders over the horse's head to protect her eyes from the dust. She turned and looked gratefully at the Shepherd.

There was difficulty in eating anything without tasting grit in every mouthful, so the Shepherd resorted to using a stick and his cloak as a make-shift tent they could eat under. Magnificent had her own feedbag, so this eliminated the problem for her.

There was stillness here in this gray dusty world; the only sound came from gusts of wind swirling the dust around. Yet Roger felt a sense of contentment in being with the Shepherd; it was that unexplainable peace he felt when he was with the Shepherd. It did not depend on the condition of the surroundings it seemed, but on the dependability of the Shepherd's nature.

So the hours passed as they alternated walking and riding, until they came to the opening of a very dark wood. This wood seemed to exude a feeling of malevolence, and if the Shepherd had not been with Roger, I don't think he could have been persuaded to enter it. He looked at it with great dread, remembering how he came through it before as a captive.

The Shepherd left Roger on the back of the horse, while he took the reins and walked, leading Magnificent into the woods. There was an eerie dripping sound that echoed as if magnified in the silence of this dark wood. There were no birds singing here and no animals seen here, but every so often, there was a slight rustling sound, as if something was furtively moving in the darkness. Roger had to almost lie down on the back of Magnificent to keep from being scratched by low-hanging branches and thorny vines winding around trees.

And then the Shepherd began to sing, and it was almost as if the song had its own tangible entity which neutralized the effect of the dismal atmosphere---and this is what he sang:

"Do not fear the darkness; it can't defeat the light---it will hide itself in shame whenever I reveal the light. The darkness is a shadow; it can't compete with light---it will vanish in the morning when I repeal the night. Fear is not reality; your hope is your security, you will find it when you seek for me with all your heart."

Roger almost had a feeling of rejoicing despite the threatening aspects of the wood and its eeriness, due to the confidence of the Shepherd even in this dark place. He could almost be grateful for the experience, since it gave him the opportunity to witness such a remarkable undaunted character as seen in the Shepherd.

"Roger," said the Shepherd as he picked his way through the murky wood, leading the horse. "Yes?" replied Roger. "Do you know what aberration means?" asked the Shepherd. "No," answered Roger. "It means a defect in a mirror which causes a distorted image," explained the Shepherd. "The evil prince uses a defective mirror to create a distorted image of reality in your mind---to disillusion you, steal your hope, and ultimately to control you. Aberration also means mental disorder---and that is the result of the enemy's goal."

"That is what they were doing to me?" asked Roger.

"Yes," said the Shepherd. "There is a battle to control what you think."

This made sense to Roger; but he wondered about those scars the Shepherd had showed him. What was that all about? He wanted to ask, but he was reluctant to bring up painful memories from the past. He knew better than to ask his dad anything about the war.

"I know you want to ask me about those scars, and I will tell you in time---but not yet," said the Shepherd.

"Waiting," thought Roger. "Everything seems to involve waiting. Why do I have to *wait* for everything?" he thought and repressed a sigh.

"I have been waiting for *you*," said the Shepherd.

Again, Roger was startled by this mind-reading characteristic of the Shepherd. There was nothing he could hide from him, he realized. No matter what he thought or felt, it would be clearly seen as if in full view. Why then did he feel so secure when with the Shepherd? It must be that sense of being accepted, regardless of what he thought or felt.

Suddenly, Roger realized that one thing the Shepherd was waiting for in him was gratefulness, instead of feeling entitled to his help. "Thank you for rescuing me," he said to the Shepherd. "I ought not to complain about anything after what you did for me."

"You are welcome," said the Shepherd, and he looked pleased.

They seemed to be nearing the end of the woods and the Shepherd began picking up sticks from those lying on the ground, until he had an armful. Just as they came out of the woods, the sun was going down and soon it was night. They could see the moon, and as the sky became darker, Roger could see more and more stars twinkling above them in the nighttime sky. The sky was a midnight navy blue, and the stars were crisp white against it.

The Shepherd had begun laying the sticks down in a pile. He started a small fire with a sharp piece of flint and a tinder box, and soon had a nice campfire blazing. He gave the horse some water, and feed, and then he and Roger sat by the fire. The Shepherd took out the last of the honey bread and some cheese and toasted this over the fire for their supper.

"Did you ever study the stars, Roger?" the Shepherd asked him. "No, not really," said Roger, since he could not remember anything from school. "People have thought of shapes and names for the different groups of stars," said the Shepherd, and he pointed out some of the constellations to Roger. They sat together by the fire, and Roger felt safe and warm.

Then the Shepherd picked up a stick that was green, and began to wrap the end of it with a long strip of cloth. Next, he poured some kind of oily substance from a flask onto the cloth, saturating it. "What is that for?" asked Roger. "Unwanted company," answered the Shepherd, as he held the cloth end over the fire until it was lit and burning with a flame.

And then Roger saw what the Shepherd meant.

Chapter 11

He saw their eyes first----their eyes were yellow, glinting in the firelight. The pack of wolves came into view; they were advancing slowly, snarling, with their fangs bared.

The Shepherd came between the wolf pack and Magnificent, holding out the torch he had made. "Roger," he said, "Untie the horse and get on her---she will take you home."

The Shepherd's tone of voice indicated that Roger did not have a choice in the matter, although he felt very unsure of riding by himself. "But what about you?" asked Roger; he was horrified at the thought of leaving the Shepherd alone with a pack of wolves.

"They will not harm me," said the Shepherd. "Don't be afraid; Magnificent knows the way and she will bring you safely home."

So Roger untied the reins and putting his foot into the stirrup, he swung his leg over and pulled himself into the saddle. Magnificent jerked her head around, turned and stamped her feet and Roger loosened the reins and let her take the lead. She began to move into a lope, and Roger leaned over and held on tightly. He turned his head to get a backward glance, and saw the Shepherd standing there holding out the blazing torch in front of the wolves.

Magnificent began to gallop, and it took all Roger's attention away from the scene behind him; he had to focus all his effort in staying on the horse by pressing with his knees, as the Shepherd had showed him. It was a terrifying ride in the darkness, but he had to trust what the Shepherd said; that the horse would bring him safely home.

Finally she began to slow her pace, and he realized that they had crossed over from the kingdom of shadows into the Kingdom of Grace. He could feel the difference in the atmosphere. He patted the horse's neck in gratitude as they continued on their journey through the night. After a while, the horse went from a trot into a walk, and Roger felt they must be very close to the Shepherd's cottage.

They had to pass through a small wood just now, however, but this one was quite different. Moonlight was lighting up the path through it, and illumined a beautiful lagoon with a small waterfall. The beams of moonlight on the waterfall made it look like sparkling jewels. Magnificent skirted this pool, and followed the path out of the woods and into a meadow. Roger saw something in the distance that looked as if it could be the Shepherd's cottage, and Magnificent was headed in that direction.

And it was; Roger sighed with relief to see that stone cottage again. He wearily dismounted and led Magnificent into the barn. He tried to remember all the things he had seen the Shepherd do for her; he went to the well and filled a bucket with water, returned to the barn and filled the trough with water, and gave her feed. He patted her and hugged her and thanked her for bringing him safely home. There was a towel hanging up, and he thought perhaps he should wipe the sweat off of the horse's coat.

So he patted her dry with this towel, and she didn't seem to mind. Then he closed the door and bolted it and turned to go to the cottage. The sheep were quiet in their pen and seemed settled for the night, also. He went inside the stone cottage, and crawled up to his place in the loft and lay down. Yet when he closed his eyes to sleep, in his mind he could still see the Shepherd standing in front of the wolf pack, holding out the torch. Finally exhaustion overtook him and he slept, despite his uneasiness over the Shepherd's welfare.

Sometime during the night, he began having a strange dream. He seemed to hear something outside, and thinking the Shepherd had come home, he went out to investigate. Instead of the Shepherd, there was a man dressed in a silver breastplate, a silver helmet with a face guard, and wearing silver gauntlets on his hands. He had a sword strapped to his side, and he stood there, looking at Roger.

Roger thought this must be the Prince, and all the pent-up anger rushed to his mind. Suddenly Roger saw a sword lying on the ground near him, and he picked it up.

"Come on," said the man in the silver armor. "I know you want to fight me. Let's duel, shall we?" he said, as he pulled out his sword from its sheath.

Roger was no swordsman; he had only his anger to motivate him, but he thrust at the man anyway. The man in armor was an excellent swordsman, and it was obvious that he was holding back so that he did not hurt Roger. He parried every blow that Roger gave, and caught Roger in a few uncomfortable positions, without cutting him. The man let him up, but Roger in his frustration, kept coming at him regardless of the fact that he was losing.

"You can't win," said the man. "Why won't you surrender to me?" And they paused in the fight for a moment and looked at each other. "Why won't you give me what I want?" Roger yelled as he lunged again, only to be blocked by the man's flat side of his sword.

"Do you think I am a genie in a lamp, and you can have your wishes granted, if you simply rub me the right way?" asked the man, as he blocked and parried Roger's insistent lunges. "You are mocking me!" yelled Roger.

"If you only knew how much I want to help you," said the man. "What is your name?" asked Roger, panting. "Why do you ask?" said the man. "I only give my name to those who submit to my authority. But it is almost morning, and I have to leave. You need to give up."

"Not until you give me a blessing!" yelled Roger, and he lunged again. "The blessing I want to give you is to change you," said the man. Roger never saw exactly how he did it, but the man flipped Roger's sword out of his hand, and pulled his arm.

Roger fell to the ground in pain; his arm was pulled out of its socket. He looked up and the man in armor was gone; he had vanished. Roger closed his eyes and groaned, and lay still.

A few moments later, he felt strong arms underneath him, picking him up. He opened his eyes and looked into the face of the Shepherd. "You're all right," he said with relief. "But you're not," said the Shepherd, and he carried Roger into the cottage and laid him down on the bed gently. Somehow the Shepherd put his arm back into its socket; Roger felt heat from the Shepherd's hands when he did this, and then the dream ended.

The next morning, Roger woke up in the loft. He opened his eyes, and remembered the dream. But was it only a dream? If so, why was his shoulder so sore? He reasoned that it must be from riding the horse; of course, that was it.

He climbed down the ladder carefully, favoring his sore arm. The Shepherd was not there, but there was his breakfast set out on the table, like all the other mornings. He went outside, and checked in the barn. Magnificent was not there either, so he surmised that the Shepherd was returning the horse to her owner. The sheep were already up on the mountain, he could see, and it looked as though another shepherd was with them.

So he went back inside, and ate his breakfast and waited. He waited for most of the morning, and still the Shepherd did not come. He became restless, and walked around outside, and there lying in the grass was a sword. He picked it up and looked at it in wonder. He put it in the cottage, leaning it against the wall in a corner of the room.

Then he went outside again, looking away into the distance. He thought of going up to talk to the shepherd up on the mountain, but since his shoulder was so sore, he decided against it. He considered walking to the village, but the thought of going alone in this countryside discouraged him from that. He remembered the bird of prey and felt helpless against such a threat. There was nothing to do but wait.

So when Roger saw that familiar figure walking up the path toward the cottage, he practically ran down the path to meet him. Without thinking, Roger hugged the Shepherd in a grateful embrace. Roger pulled back in embarrassment, but when he saw the expression of delight on the Shepherd's face, he was then glad for his display of affection, however indiscreet it may have been. They continued walking together, back toward the stone cottage.

"I had something made for you," said the Shepherd. "But I think some clean clothes and washing up are first in order."

Roger looked down at his very dirty, blood-stained clothes he had been in for several days now. He had not even thought about it, but now he realized he smelled, and he grinned. So after thoroughly washing up and putting on yet another set of clothing from his unknown friend, Roger put on the arm sling that the Shepherd gave him.

Then they talked about the sword that Roger had found. He showed it to the Shepherd and said, "I thought it was all a dream until I found this in the grass." The Shepherd adjusted Roger's arm sling, and said, "No more fighting for *you* for a while."

Roger smiled sheepishly and answered, "I was very foolish to try to fight him, whoever he is."

Chapter 12

Roger and the Shepherd ate their noon meal together at the Shepherd's table. Roger asked who had made the sling for him, and the Shepherd said it was a woman from the village.

"In fact," said the Shepherd, "She is the mother of your benefactor."

"My what?" asked Roger, "What is a benefactor?"

"The one who blessed you with these clothes," the Shepherd said, "And I would like to take you to meet him this afternoon."

So after they finished their meal, they set out to go to the village. It was a beautiful afternoon, and there were no mishaps or threatening occurrences along the way. They walked through the rocky meadow and then came to the path leading to the brook. After crossing over the bridge with its musical waters below, they came to the path under the trees. Finally they arrived at the border of blue spruce trees surrounding the castle grounds. They passed through this, and soon came to the village.

Everyone who was outside at the time, stopped whatever they happened to be doing to greet the

Shepherd and Roger as they walked through the village. They arrived at last at a small cottage on the outskirts of the village. A young man who looked to be about Roger's age was outside the cottage, and greeted them heartily. He went inside, and told his mother they were here, and she came outside and welcomed them in.

"Roger," said the Shepherd, "this is Abel, the young man I told you about." Roger and Abel looked at each other, and Roger immediately liked him. His candor and frankness were apparent in his countenance. They were almost the same size, though Abel was slightly older. Abel's mother was happy to see that the sling she had made was helping Roger. (And no one asked how he got this particular injury, for which Roger was very thankful) Roger was profusely apologetic that he did not have the other set of clothes with him to return them; they were soaking in a bucket of sudsy water in hopes they might be able to remove the stains. Abel's mother, whose name was Lydia, did not seem overly concerned, and merely said, "It will be all right."

Abel had a sister who was a year younger than he, and her name was Rhoda. He also had a much younger brother and sister, whose names were Simeon and Phoebe. Their house and its furnishings were very simple; it reminded Roger of the prairie homes of the 1800's in his own country. There was a large open area with a kitchen on one side, and a fireplace against another wall, and a large rough wooden table in the center with benches along the sides, and two chairs on either end. The only other furnishings in this room were a cupboard, a desk, and a rocking chair. There was a bedroom with a loft, and a smaller bedroom on the side of this. The rough wooden interior walls were painted white, and the curtains were bright colors. Combined with a few colorful wall hangings, these had a cheery effect.

The children's schooling was finished for the day, and Abel asked Roger if he would like to see his father's shop before it was closed down for the day. Abel's father was a blacksmith, as well as a bladesmith. "What is the difference?" Roger wanted to know as they walked to the shop. "None really," said Abel. "They use many of the same tools, but a bladesmith is known for making knives and swords, and a blacksmith makes a variety of things like nails, bolts, sickles, axes, hammers, wheel rims, and horseshoes. My father does both."

At the shop, Roger watched in fascination as Abel's father held a piece of metal with tongs, heating it in a forge, and then beat it into a shape with different kinds of hammers on an anvil. He used a chisel and a punch tool to further shape it. Next, he quenched it in a bucket of water, and then filed it with a rasp so the edges were smooth. The result was a large metal hook; it would be used in a barn to hang up a harness.

It was almost time for the evening meal, so Abel's father prepared to close up his shop. His name was Asa, Roger learned on their way back to their home, and he had been tutored in blacksmithing by his father. Abel would soon start learning the trade as well.

They arrived back at the cottage, and the Shepherd was telling stories to Abel's younger brother and sister. They were spellbound by the Shepherd's animated tale of a young shepherd who fought off a lion and a bear. Rhoda was helping her mother prepare the food.

And then it was time for the evening meal, and the family sat down together at the rough wooden table. The Shepherd blessed the food, and then all the serving dishes were passed around and each one filled their plate. Abel's mother had to help the younger children, of course, so they were sitting near her. Roger looked around wistfully at this family; there was so much joy and affection shared between them, and it caused a longing in him. His own family life had been so fraught with tension and anxiety, that it was chaotic.

After the meal, all of the children (including Roger) helped clear the table and wash the dishes. Then Abel's mother insisted on finishing the job, and told the younger children to go and prepare for bed, leaving the older children to visit together a little longer. So Abel, Roger, and Rhoda went outside while the Shepherd and Asa talked together.

"So what do you do for fun?" asked Roger. "Oh, we swordfight," said Abel and he grinned. He went in their barn and returned with two blunted swords. "These are dull on purpose so we can practice," he told Roger. Rhoda and Abel had a lively duel, while Roger watched with great interest. After they stopped, Abel asked Roger about his life, and what he did for fun. "Nothing much," said Roger, trying to remember. "Mostly computer games," he said.

"What is that?" asked Rhoda, but Roger had no idea of how to explain this. He simply answered that it was a very complicated type of game board. "Well, we can make game boards on the ground here," said Rhoda. "We use sticks and rocks." And she proceeded to show him a game that seemed similar to tic-tac-toe. Abel showed Roger a homemade ball, which he said they used for football; but the game sounded to Roger as more like soccer. It involved a lot more footwork and no handling of the ball or tackling one's opponents.

Presently the Shepherd came out and said that they must return home now. Roger thanked Abel's parents for their hospitality, and said goodbye to his friends. And so he and the Shepherd began the walk home. It was dark by now, but the stars were out and it was a beautiful night to be outside.

It was refreshingly cool, and there was a delightful smell. "What is that smell?" asked Roger. "It's the blooms on the sweet olive trees," replied the Shepherd. The smell was very strong here near the village, and Roger saw the trees that the Shepherd meant.

They walked past a few small farms and cottages, and then came to the tall blue spruce trees, and these also had a smell that reminded Roger of Christmas. This smell only belonged to some very faded childhood Christmas memories, from when he was quite young. His father and mother were much happier then, and his sister was only a baby at that time. Things were so different now, that they barely celebrated Christmas.

"Roger," said the Shepherd, "What did you think of Abel?"

Roger looked at the Shepherd and smiled. "I know you know my thoughts; why do you ask? Yes, I like him a lot."

"Good," said the Shepherd. "You have needed a friend."

"I guess so," answered Roger. "We have moved so often, that I don't really make friends."

"I also noticed how much you enjoyed being with his family," said the Shepherd. "Would you like to stay with his family for a while?"

This was very tempting to Roger; he really liked the idea. But there was something that he wanted even more than this. "Yes, I would like that," said Roger, "But if it's okay, I would rather stay with you."

"Eventually you will have to return home," said the Shepherd. "Your mother will need you."

"I don't want to go home," said Roger. "Could you bring my mother here?"

"Why don't you want to go home?" asked the Shepherd gently.

"I want to stay with you----forever. I'll do anything you want, just let me stay with you," pleaded Roger earnestly.

"Anything?" asked the Shepherd, looking at Roger intently.

"Yes, anything," said Roger emphatically. "When you were gone, and I didn't know what had happened to you with the wolf pack and all that, I realized how much I missed you. I don't want to be separated from you---ever."

"I'm really glad to hear you say that, Roger," said the Shepherd, "especially if you mean that part about doing anything." "I do mean that," said Roger. "I will do anything you want me to."

Chapter 13

Roger looked at the Shepherd's face after this declaration, and he thought he caught a glimpse of some kind of radiance, emanating from the Shepherd's face---as if light was coming out of him. Then it was gone, and Roger wondered if he imagined it, after all.

They continued on the journey home; Roger asked about Magnificent, and the Shepherd said he had returned her to the castle. Roger immediately wondered who she belonged to, and the Shepherd explained that she was the property of the Prince, but he was allowed to ride her whenever he needed a horse.

Roger didn't say anything, but he thought that this was very gracious of the Prince. The Shepherd asked with a smile, "Does that make you like the Prince a little more?" And Roger had to admit it did. "Good," said the Shepherd, and he smiled to himself.

When they arrived at the Shepherd's cottage, it was getting late, and the Shepherd sent Roger to the loft to get enough rest for the next day. "Tomorrow will be a special day for you," he said. Roger didn't resist at all; he was still tired from the ordeal he had been through. The cuts on his back were healing well; the Shepherd had put ointment on them each day, and now they didn't bother him so much anymore.

The bedding had been washed and dried, and so he had a very comfortable sleep that night in blankets that smelled fresh and clean. And his shoulder was not nearly so sore as before. He was quite content in his loft bed, looking out at the stars through the round window over him. He was with the Shepherd; and that was the best part of all, he thought, and he fell asleep.

He woke up early enough to meet the other shepherd who was bringing the sheep up to the mountain. This shepherd had very brown skin, straight, thick black hair and eyebrows, and he sang in a robust voice with a rich vibrato. This is what Roger heard him singing: "We are the sheep of his pasture; we belong to him; he calls us by name and we come to him. No danger by night, no terror by day can harm us at all when we follow his way." He stopped to greet Roger and introduce himself; his name was Phillip. Then he began walking toward the mountain, and all the sheep followed him as he went, with bleating and bells tinkling. This scene was like an illustration out of a storybook, in Roger's mind, and he relished it. He stood there watching until the entire flock had passed by him, and then he went inside.

The Shepherd had breakfast ready, and seemed very eager and excited today. Roger ate and got dressed, and the Shepherd helped him put the sling on his arm. Then the Shepherd got his shoulder bag and provisions and his staff, and they left the cottage and began walking toward the meadow.

"Where are we going?" asked Roger.

"Today is the day you will meet the Prince," said the Shepherd, "and I have been looking forward to this day."

Roger stopped. "But I don't want to meet the Prince," he protested.

"Are you going to go back on your word to me?" asked the Shepherd. "You told me last night that you would do anything I wanted in order to stay with me. Now will you trust me?"

Roger reluctantly agreed, but he was disappointed. He had no more interest in meeting the Prince, now that he realized how much he wanted to be with the Shepherd. He didn't want to stay at the castle and be parted from the Shepherd, and this concerned him greatly.

Yet Roger went on without any more complaints, since this was what the Shepherd wanted, and it obviously pleased him. Everything around him seemed to be rejoicing, too; the birds were singing many different songs, and the butterflies were in abundance, serenely floating over the flower heads. The brook played its music as they crossed, and the animals in the woods shyly watched them as they went by.

The Shepherd and Roger picked some of the fruit under the trees here, and ate it, and a little mongoose type creature retrieved the peelings and took them into its hole in the ground. Roger had not seen this happen before, and he thought of how much Sundae would enjoy seeing that. He had not thought of her for days, and he felt a little guilty. Maybe it was a good thing that he was going to the castle, after all, he thought to himself. He quickly looked at the Shepherd as he thought this, for he knew the Shepherd would know his thoughts---but there was no change in the Shepherd's expression.

They turned toward the path that led to the castle, and went through the meadows here, and then through the border of blue spruce trees. When they came to the village, the Shepherd went to the bakery and got two large soft baked pretzels for himself and Roger. They found a resting place under a tree nearby and sat down to eat these. There was also a well close by and they drank from the dipper.

Then the Shepherd turned to go toward the castle, and Roger walked alongside him, dreading this last part of the journey. They came to the colored stone walkway and Roger was very quiet as they walked, remembering the last time he had been here in this place. Together they walked up the brick steps which led to the walled corridor they must go through, to get to the entrance of the castle, and the gate of the corridor opened by itself as if expecting them.

They went through the walled corridor, and then Roger saw the words which were carved above the massive arched doors of the castle, and these words glowed like fire. This is what Roger read: NOTHING IMPURE MAY DWELL HERE.

Roger looked at the Shepherd with a hurt expression; he felt betrayed. This was not the welcome he had hoped for; this spelled more rejection. He knew that he was not pure, and it was unfair, because he didn't know how to make himself pure.

"I thought you were going to prepare me," he said to the Shepherd. "I'm not ready for this."

"Do it for me," said the Shepherd. "Go in because I want you to."

"Are you coming with me?" asked Roger, and he was dismayed to hear the Shepherd say that he would not be going in; that Roger would have to go alone.

Roger almost refused to go in, after hearing that; but the Shepherd told Roger that if he went inside, he would soon see how he truly was granting Roger's request to be with him.

The Shepherd turned and began walking away through the corridor, and Roger had the impulse to run after him and beg to go with him; but he restrained himself and stood staring at the door, trying to muster up the resolve to knock. When he turned around to look once more at the departing Shepherd, there was no one there.

So at last he knocked, and a woman opened the door and stood there smiling at him. She invited him in, and led him down a hallway to a small round room. This must be a type of waiting room, he thought to himself, as he looked around at its furnishings. There were soft velvet chairs, and tables, and books to look at were spread on the tables. "Wait here," the woman said kindly, "I will bring you something to drink, and let the Prince know that you have arrived."

Roger sat down, and began looking at the books. Suddenly, he was very shocked to see a likeness of a younger version of Mr. Rusty on the cover of one of these books. He became absorbed in reading the narrative in this little book; it told how the Prince had rescued Rusty as a young boy and how he adopted Rusty and gave him a new life. Then he saw another book, and it had to be a picture of Pearl as a young girl, and he read about her story. It was very similar to Rusty's story; she too had been an orphan, and the Prince adopted her and loved her as his own child.

The woman came back with a glass of mint tea and a plate of pastries and set these down on one of the tables that did not have any books. "I will be back soon to bring you to the Prince," she said as she left the room.

Roger liked the tea and the pastries, whatever they were. He suddenly noticed a gold book on a taller table close to the wall; this book looked as if it were glowing. He walked over to this, and looked at its open page. He read the words, but he was not sure of the meaning. While he was puzzling over this, the woman came back to escort him to the throne room.

"I was told that I needed to be prepared for this, but I'm not sure if I am," said Roger to the woman.

"Can you tell me what I'm supposed to do when I meet him?" he asked.

"Do not worry," she assured Roger. "The Shepherd would not have brought you to the Prince if he did not think that you were ready. When you meet the Prince, you will understand many things that you could not before. So come, and I will take you to meet him," she said and indicated that Roger should follow her. He got up and walked out of the waiting room.

Chapter 14

The first thing that he noticed as he walked down this long hallway was the many lights on its ceiling which twinkled like stars. Then he saw on either side of them that the walls had life-size life-like paintings of trees, animals and birds. These seemed to watch him solemnly as he passed by, and it seemed that they followed him with their eyes. Yet it wasn't an eerie feeling; and the paintings themselves were very beautiful and skillfully done. He was very inspired by these, and it kept him from having as much apprehension as he might have experienced.

He followed the woman all the way down this hallway until they came to the doors of the throne room of the Prince. Here she stopped and smiled at him in a reassuring manner, and then she opened the doors.

It was with a great shock that Roger looked in and saw the grandeur of this room. It was more resplendent than anything he could have imagined. There were the huge arching windows with white filmy curtains, tied back with gold cords, the elaborate frescoed golden ceiling with many glass chandeliers; the tile floor with its red, blue, and gold designs; the white arches and white pillars decorated with scrollwork at top and bottom, and a huge white marble platform for the throne.

And then he saw the Prince. The face of this personage was so aglow that at first he could not distinguish his features. There was a light coming from within this person; it was shining out of his face, and his royal clothes had a luminance as well.

Mercy, the doorkeeper, (for that was her name) beckoned Roger to step in and he did. Then he saw Sundae standing by the woman named Saphire, and she waved to him excitedly.

The Prince said, "Come to me, Roger." Roger heard this as if in a "fog" and there was something familiar about this voice, but he could not detect what it was. Mercy indicated that it was all right for him to go closer, and he began to walk toward the white marble throne upon the platform. He was afraid at first, but with every step forward he felt less and less afraid. And then he reached the bottom of the platform, and the Prince stood up.

"Roger," said the Prince, "Will you do what I want so that we can be together forever?"

"Who are you?" asked Roger in confusion.

"I am the Shepherd," said the Prince. "And I am also a warrior." As he said these last words, one of the Prince's attendants standing near him showed Roger the silver helmet and sword.

Roger was speechless. "Come closer to me," said the Prince. And Roger stepped up on the platform of the throne, and the Prince stepped down one step so that they were closer to each other, and Roger looked into those deep blue eyes that were like the ocean.

"Roger," said the Prince. "You were like a "bummer lamb"---rejected by its parent, and I had to keep you close to me as a shepherd does, so that you would learn to trust me."

Roger could hardly take any of this in; he was baffled and mesmerized at the same time. "Why did you let me fight you?" he finally was able to ask.

"You thought of me as a foe, and you were fighting me inside; I had to make you see that I don't want to harm you."

"But.....you pulled my arm out of socket.....why?" asked a very perplexed Roger.

"It was part of my plan to help you surrender to me, Roger," said the Prince. "Now take off your sling."

Roger did, and discovered that there was free movement again in his arm and shoulder, without any soreness at all. An attendant took the sling from him, and he gladly gave it up.

"Roger, I want you to be with me forever--- as much and more than you want to be with me. But there is something which prevents that---and it is the sickness inside you. I have the antidote for this sickness in my blood---but in order for me to heal you, you must surrender your life completely to me," said the Prince.

"What is this sickness?" asked Roger in bewilderment.

"It is the thing which makes you impure; it is the malady of sin," said the Prince. "I told you that I would explain those scars that I showed you, and today I will do that." The Prince removed his royal tunic and everyone could see those deep scars on his upper torso. "Come, Roger---touch these scars," said the Prince, and he came even closer to Roger.

Roger reached out his hand and touched one of those deep scars. Instantly, the room began to whirl, and he felt as though he was in a swirling cloud of some sort; and then he was in another place. He saw the Prince and men were hurling something at him, and these men were behaving like animals and snarling at him and jeering and laughing. The prince was against a wall; there were spikes protruding from his chest and blood was pouring out of him onto the ground. And the men laughed and threw their stones at him and crushed his bones until he died. When he was dead, they threw his body over the wall, and they left.

The vision ended, and Roger felt as if he was transported back through clouds into the throne room again. He was in a daze, but he managed to say, "You're alive…" and he touched the warm body of the Prince again in amazement.

"Yes, I am alive. My Father is king of the universe; his power is greater than death and he gave my life back to me. But I died to pay the penalty for the crime which began this sickness, and to obtain the antidote," answered the Prince.

The Prince put his tunic on again, and looked at Roger. "If you surrender your life to me, we can be together forever. I will always be there for you; you can depend on me forever."

Roger went down on one knee before the Prince. "I surrender," he said.

There was such a sound of jubilation in the throne room from all those who witnessed this, that it sounded like a roar in Roger's ears. Roger stood up and said, "Now what do I do?"

The Prince said, "There will be a ceremony this very afternoon. Mercy will show you how to be prepared for that, and I will see you in a little while." The Prince smiled at Roger, and it was like beams of light went all over the room from that smile.

Roger looked around for Mercy and she asked him to follow her, and Roger did but he stopped when he saw Sundae. "Just a moment, please," he asked Mercy, and she waited.

"Isn't he wonderful?" asked Sundae, looking up at her brother's face. "Yes," said Roger. "And all that time, I was with him, and didn't even know it--- because he is the shepherd, too." Roger hugged his sister tightly, and then released her and began to walk with Mercy out of the room.

Mercy led Roger to the bathing rooms, where he was able to take a warm shower, and there was a set of very fine clothes and shoes for him to wear, set out for him in this room. When he was dressed and ready, Mercy came to escort him back to the throne room.

The throne room was filled with many witnesses; Sundae and Saphire were there as well, waiting joyfully. Roger walked in with Mercy right beside him, and waited. The Prince was sitting on his throne and he was holding a scepter. "Come, Roger," he said. "I have been waiting for this day, and I am so glad it is here." He smiled and light seemed to come from him, radiating all around the room.

Roger went to the throne platform and waited. The Prince stood and stepped down until he was closer to Roger. He looked at Roger with such love and compassion in his eyes, that Roger's eyes began to fill with tears. He had never felt so loved before in his entire life.

"Roger, do you trust in my antidote and that I can change you?" asked the Prince.

"Yes, I do----and I am so grateful for all you have done for me," said Roger. "You have cared for me and loved me, even when I resisted you and resented you. You rescued me even though I had rebelled against you. Now that I know you, I don't want to live without having you in my life."

"All you need to do now is touch my scepter," said the Prince, and he held it out to Roger.

Roger touched it, and light flashed all around the throne area with a brilliance that made Roger close his eyes. When he opened them again, he saw the tears of joy in the Prince's eyes, and the Prince held his arms open wide to Roger. Roger put his arms around the Prince and put his head on his chest and the Prince held Roger in his arms.

I think that there were many tears of joy in the throne room that day.

Chapter 15

The Prince introduced Roger to all the people in the throne room as his new son and heir to the Kingdom of Grace, and he presented Roger with a ring that had the royal insignia of the Prince's Kingdom. Then two books were brought in and put on pedestals, and the Prince explained that Roger's name was now inscribed in his book of heirs of the kingdom.

The other book was the gold book that Roger had looked at before in the waiting room. The Prince asked Roger to look at this book, and this time Roger understood the meaning! This was a book of promises from the Prince and his father, to all their adopted children.

"For you see, Roger," said the Prince, "When I adopt you, my father does too. You now belong to both of us. I would like to introduce you to another member of my immediate family: Sir Guide. He is as much a part of me as I am of my father, and he will be your trainer and teacher, as well."

Sir Guide stepped forward and embraced Roger. "Welcome into our family," he said with a huge beaming smile, and then he stepped back, for the Prince's next part of the ceremony.

The Prince sang his song to Roger, and these were the words: "I have loved you from the dawn of time, long before the world began; I have known you in your mother's womb---I have called you by your name."

Roger remembered when he first heard these words; the shepherd was singing this song on the way home to the stone cottage the first day he was with the shepherd. How little he understood then! Now Roger believed the words, and knew they were for him; and suddenly he realized they were for his sister, his mother---- and his father, too.

The Prince beckoned to Sundae to come, and then he sang the song again to both Roger and Sundae. Roger hugged his sister and kissed her on the top of her head, and when the song was ended, he told her quietly, "I'm so sorry, Sundae, and I love you." Sundae looked up at him, and said, "I'm so happy you came," and she hugged him tightly.

Then the Prince announced that there would be a reception on the lawn and everyone could begin to make their way outside to the lawn of the castle. Roger was stopped on the way and congratulated by so many people that he was overwhelmed at the attention, but it was so heartfelt and genuine that he could not help but be encouraged by the response.

Finally they were outside and as it was early evening by then, there were many lanterns on stands all around the castle grounds and white cloth covered tables were arranged neatly on the lawn. There were centerpieces of flowers on each one; and platters of sandwiches and fruits and desserts equally as lovely, were on each table. The Prince had a table on a raised dais and there were seats for Roger and Sundae next to him at this table. The Prince invited Abel to come and sit by Roger, and he did so, and Saphire came to sit by Sundae.

Cedric said the blessing over the food, and then everyone began eating, but Cedric came to the Prince's table and asked Roger about his friends Rusty and Pearl. Roger told about their shop and how happy they were, and how they had helped him and Sundae. Cedric was excited to hear all of this, and then he asked if there was a small black metal birdcage in the shop, by any chance; and when Roger said yes, Cedric laughed and laughed. Roger looked so puzzled, and Cedric promised he would tell him the story of that birdcage one day.

The moon was very large and white that night, sharing its light generously over the castle grounds; and shining on this party. Even all the stars seemed to be rejoicing at this happy occasion, Roger thought to himself. The thought occurred to him that maybe even all of creation groaned and waited for people to become who they were meant to be; the children of the Prince and his father. He turned to the Prince and said, "I can't thank you enough for all you did to help me give my life to you. I can't even begin to thank you for what you did to get the antidote for us."

Roger looked into those deep blue eyes, and he saw that what he said pleased the Prince. And then he told the Prince something that had been hard for him to say to any adult, especially a man: he said, "I love you."

Light began to shine from the Prince's face and he said, "I love you, Roger. I will never stop loving you, and nothing will ever be able to separate you from my love."

And then the Prince invited Roger, Abel, and Sundae to see his river; Saphire followed too, as they went through the castle to the other side and saw a river as blue as the Prince's eyes. The Prince explained that this was a place of refreshing; they could swim here anytime they wanted, but especially when they were weary or discouraged and they would be inspired.

Sundae asked if they could try it now, and the Prince gave permission. So Roger and Abel and Sundae took off their shoes and ran down to the river. They slowly stepped in, and the water was so blue--yet so clear--that they could see everything even underwater. There was so much moonlight that the water was illuminated, and there were lanterns all along the shore as well. The children swam and splashed and played and even Saphire couldn't resist it and she joined them. The Prince stood on the shore watching their play, amused with their antics. When it was time to get out of the water, the children discovered that their clothes and hair were immediately dry again.

They were so surprised, and asked how it could be so; but the Prince merely smiled and said it was how he wanted it to be for them. And then he told them that he had many other surprises in store for them at the castle; and when they went back, they found it was so.

There was a room prepared especially for Roger; and it was right next to Sundae's room. There were pajamas in the room for him, and several changes of clothes; but the best part was that the ceiling of the room was decorated with a large mural of the stars. It was just as if he were looking out of the little round window in the shepherd's cottage, but on a much grander scale.

Abel admired Roger's room very much, and the Prince invited him to come and spend time with Roger when he was not engaged with his family activities. "In fact," said the Prince with a smile, "I have something planned for you both with Sir Guide. But tomorrow, I need to show you my garden."

Roger and Sundae went with Abel to the lawn again, and greeted his family members, and then Abel and his family left to go to their home. Roger and Sundae went back to their new rooms in the castle and the Prince presented Roger with his own copy of the gold book. (Sundae already had hers, and had been reading it)

So Roger spent his first night at the castle, reading the promises of the Prince until he fell asleep. There were no nightmares here either; the only thing he missed was that he was not sharing a room with the "Shepherd", who he now knew as the Prince. Yet he was both prince and shepherd; and Roger realized now that in knowing him, he had everything that he had ever needed or wanted. The Prince was near, and that was enough.

The next morning, when Roger woke up, he felt the strangest sensation. It was as if he had just been born, and he was waking up to his real life. He could hear the birds singing more clearly than ever before; he looked out the window and the grass was greener and the flowers were brighter in color than ever before. He got dressed and went out into a large hallway that was like a lobby, and there was a table and chairs by the large windows overlooking a garden. Sundae was sitting at this table waiting for him. Suddenly, he realized that he loved her more than he ever had, and appreciated that he had a sister. He went and sat by her and looked at her. She was no longer just a duty and a burden to him; he realized that she was a gift to him, and he was grateful.

This time as she talked to him, he really listened and admired her creativity and her imagination. She was funny, and winsome, and he wanted to write down everything she said and remember it. How had he missed seeing this before?

Mercy brought them some breakfast, and sat with them for a few moments enjoying their company and making them feel truly welcomed and special.

Then Roger looked out at the garden and he saw the Prince, and he had an overwhelming sense of joy to see the one who loved him so much----and had pursued him until he could love him back. "Would it be alright if I go ahead into the garden?" he asked Mercy hesitantly, for he recognized that he must also reverence the Prince as a sovereign royal ruler.

Mercy answered that the Prince was waiting for Roger, and would be delighted if Roger joined him. Roger needed no further encouragement, and he went quickly down to the garden where the Prince stood among the aisles of flowers and ornamental trees.

Roger could think of nothing better at this moment than spending time with the Prince. He was rewarded with the look of ecstasy on the face of the Prince when he saw Roger approaching. Roger knew that this was what it really meant to be home: to be loved like this.

Chapter 16

Roger and the Prince met every day in the garden to talk, and the Prince shared many things with Roger to help him grow in his knowledge of the Kingdom of Grace.

The Prince had such an understanding of the ways of humankind, though he came from a world far away in the heavens, and he had unending compassion for people who were like sheep without a shepherd. They were ravaged by anger and hurt and selfishness and greed.

The Prince told many stories to Roger and his sister that explained how the truth had been twisted in the minds of humankind because of the malady within. Reality was opposite to the things that people had imagined and believed and lived for.

Though he was a prince, he taught Roger and Sundae about seeds and soil, and together they planted flowers in the garden and tended them. This was a new experience for these children; they had moved so often that there was never enough time for such things as a garden. Roger and Sundae were delighted to see life spring up from the seeds they planted. And it was as if new hope was planted in their hearts, as well. They began to believe in miracles in a way that they never had before.

This was of course, the Prince's doings, for he was with them and they were changing as they spent time with him. But there was this one lingering question that Roger wanted to ask; and finally one day, he did.

"There is a question you want to ask me," said the Prince to Roger, one day when Sundae was not with them. "Yes," said Roger. "I still don't understand why you pulled my arm out of socket that night. Why did you hurt me?"

The prince's face looked sad at that moment as he answered, "I take no pleasure in causing you----or anyone----pain. I would far rather heal you than hurt you, for when you are in pain, I am in grief too because of my love for you. But I will do whatever it takes to win you over to me, and sometimes pain is the only way I can rescue you from rebelling against me and falling further into the trap of the evil one."

The Prince looked intently at Roger to see if he understood, but Roger was still puzzled. "Pain causes vulnerability and need," said the Prince. "Humankind is proud to be self-sufficient and does not look for help without the humility that pain brings."

The Prince went on to say: "Until they are confronted with the knowledge of the disease that is destroying them, they do not even realize that anything is wrong. Since they have always been in this condition, they do not know that there is a sickness."

"That is how it was with me," said Roger, comprehending this truth. "I always blamed my unhappiness on my father, but there was something wrong inside me, too."

"Roger," said the Prince, "You will soon become a man....and later a father yourself. Sir Guide is going to begin training you, for every man must become a warrior to fight evil."

Abel joined Roger in these training sessions, and Roger was grateful to have a comrade. Their training began with simple exercises of climbing, running, and jumping, which gradually became more strenuous and more challenging. Roger imagined that this must be something like a military "boot camp", though he had heard that the officers there were often crude. Sir Guide was neither crude nor harsh, though he was firm. Sir Guide expected obedience, but Roger observed that there was pleasure and satisfaction in yielding to his commands. Whenever Roger resisted the challenge, he felt sad because it was disappointing to Sir Guide. Since he did not like that feeling, Roger resolved to acquiesce more diligently and respect every request given. He was rewarded with an even greater satisfaction.

Their training progressed to swordsmanship, and Roger was very excited. He and Abel began to practice using rounded wooden swords. Roger was beginning to understand how crucial the climbing, running, and jumping was for preparation in sword combat. Now he was grateful for the regimen that Sir Guide had put them through, and that they were continuing. He had not realized how much energy it took to wield a sword and fight with one. And they had not even begun to use metal swords!

Then there was armor that would have to be worn; but Sir Guide did not want to weigh them down with too much at one time, so they would gradually become used to each piece of armor. They began with the helmet. Sir Guide said this was first because it protected the head; he alluded to the Prince's antidote as protection for the mind and explained that this is what the helmet represented.

Sundae had a much different sort of training with Sir Guide. She and a few other girls were learning to dance, under Sir Guide's instruction. At first, Sundae was confused about this; she thought it very strange that dancing would be part of the Kingdom of Grace. Sir Guide explained that the original purpose of dancing was not allurement or enticement or anything of that nature; it was to celebrate the goodness of the Kingdom of Grace. Dancing here was an expression of gratitude for the love of the Prince for his people.

Sundae absorbed that quietly and was thinking on this, when she remembered something that made her sad. She had been to a wedding, and the father of the bride had danced with his daughter all around the room. Some tears welled up in her eyes and began to roll down her cheeks. Sir Guide went and sat beside her and took her hand in his.

She looked up at him and said, "I don't think I will ever get to dance with my father." Sir Guide said, "I know a secret. The Prince told me that there is a certain little girl who is learning how to dance, and he plans to personally dance with her as her father, in the very near future."

Sundae was full of awe at that thought, and looked up at Sir Guide with wonder in her eyes. "I guess I had better learn quickly!" she told Sir Guide, and he smiled at her exuberance.

Sundae was also learning how to bake; this is something she had yearned to do with her mother, but their circumstances had not allowed them to enjoy this activity together. A lady named Isabella was her instructor, and together they made cookies with different shapes and decorations, and cakes with frosting, and even the special scones which were served to visitors at the palace.

Saphire also was teaching Sundae about sewing, and Sundae made an apron to wear while baking, and embroidered her own name on the pocket.

There were times of music instruction, and Sundae and Roger learned the songs of the Kingdom of Grace. Sundae overcame her shyness about singing, and Roger surprised himself with his aptitude for playing bongos. He had never had any experience at all with music or instruments.

These children had never had any art instruction, and they responded to this with great enthusiasm. Roger enjoyed making things out of wood, and Sundae liked painting in water colors. The restraints and misgivings which usually hinder people from the confidence to try new things were not present in this place.

Even with all of this going on, there was still time for games and swimming and picnics.

Roger and Abel had advanced in their training in wearing all of the armor; they were each outfitted with the helmet, breastplate, belt, and shoes. Then came the day when they began using the shields and the metal swords. (These swords were still blunted for their safety) Sir Guide had carefully explained the meaning of each piece of armor to the young men. The breastplate represented the goodness of the Kingdom of Grace which protected the heart; the belt represented the truth of the Prince's promises, and the shoes represented the willingness to go and rescue others from the evil prince. The shield represented the protection of the Prince for his children, and the sword represented his power against evil.

There were times of great celebration at the castle, and the people of the Kingdom of Grace acted out stories which showed how the Prince cared for his children and his people. One evening, one of these plays was presented and Roger and Abel acted in it as warriors wearing their armor and having a mock duel. The audience reacted with much applause.

And after the play, the musicians gathered and played a rousing waltz rather like a Celtic song. The Prince called for Sundae, who had been dressed in a long full ball gown for this occasion.

(Although she did not know why) The Prince took her hand, and gallantly waltzed her all around the entire length of the large meeting room while everyone stood back and watched. There was never a more delighted little girl than Sundae that night!

Another surprise awaited Roger; Sir Guide told him that the next part of their training would involve horses. Roger could hardly sleep that night, he was so elated.

Sundae slept very deeply, but she dreamed of dancing with the Prince.

Chapter 17

The next morning, after breakfast and the time devoted to reading the gold book of promises, Sir Guide came to escort Roger to a large enclosed pasture. There Roger saw a beautiful sight in the morning sunshine; it was a golden tan mare with a creamy white mane. She pranced and shook her long white mane as if the morning air energized her.

"What is her name?" Roger asked, and Sir Guide told him that it was Sunrise. Just then a black and white horse with a white star on her forehead came out of the stable into the sunshine and began running around the outer perimeter of the enclosure. Her mane waved in the wind, her legs moved in an elegant rhythm, and she ran as if she was rejoicing in life itself. Roger's eyes followed her around the ellipse of the enclosure as she ran. There was a light sparkling in Sir Guide's eyes; it was a reflection of the joy he saw in Roger's eyes at this sight. "Who is that?" asked Roger, without taking his eyes off the horse.

"Starlight," said Sir Guide with a radiant smile. "She will be yours."

Roger was so astonished that he didn't know what to say. Finally he managed to say, "Really?" "Yes," answered Sir Guide. "Yes, she is for you.....but you will have to learn how to ride her and care for her. Then you will learn how to ride her while wearing your armor."

Roger finally turned and looked at Sir Guide in surprise. "What....kind of horse is she?" he asked. Sir Guide replied, "I think in your world, she would be called a "paint" horse. That is the breed especially known by their coloring. Here, she is actually a warhorse."

"What makes her a warhorse?" Roger asked. "A warhorse," said Sir Guide, "is a horse that has become meek and now has courage and confidence to go into battle with its master."

Roger looked confused. "Ah, yes," said Sir Guide. "I know that look. The word meek does not mean the same thing in your world as it used to mean."

"I thought meek meant shy and timid and sort of....weak," said Roger.

"That is what people in your world think that it means now," said Sir Guide. "The original meaning is very different; it is derived from the Greek word *praus*. This is the word the Greeks used to describe a warhorse that has been trained to respond to its master at the slightest touch or command. That type of horse has such a relationship of trust with its master that it is obedient and yet still very high-spirited and strong."

"So becoming meek means the horse has been trained like that," Roger stated, waiting for confirmation from Sir Guide. "Yes," said Sir Guide. "That is right. The Prince trained Magnificent to be a warhorse, and she is extremely valuable because of her obedience."

"She took me all the way home while the Prince held off a pack of wolves," said Roger admiringly.

"She is very trustworthy," agreed Sir Guide. "Her spirit is bonded to the Prince because of love. She would lay down her life for him if that is what he wanted."

"That would definitely take a lot of courage!" exclaimed Roger.

"Yes," said Sir Guide. "And that is the true meaning of meekness---it is a loyal courage springing from a bond of love. The Prince himself is very meek."

"The Prince?" Roger questioned. "He has no master."

"No," said Sir Guide. "But when his father asked him to sacrifice his life to obtain the antidote, he was obedient even unto death. That took great courage; that is meekness."

Just then, someone approached the enclosure, and as this person came within view, Roger was delighted to see that it was Abel.

"Now we are ready to begin your riding lessons. Abel will be riding Sunrise, " said Sir Guide jovially, and he led the way to the stable. Sir Guide showed the boys the different stalls and rooms in the stable, and where the saddles and harnesses were kept. Their first lesson would be to learn how to put the saddle and bridle on their horses properly. And now we shall leave them to their lessons, and view what Sundae has been doing.

Sundae had not been idle. When the morning light burst into her room, Sundae dressed and wanted to go immediately down into the gardens and walk among all the flowers. Mercy would not allow this, and Sundae resisted this restraint. Mercy told her gently that she must eat her breakfast and read in the gold book of promises before she did anything else.

"But I read it yesterday!" protested Sundae. "Yes," said Mercy, "but that has already been used up in yesterday. You need a fresh hope for today."

"Yes, ma'am," said Sundae compliantly, although she still fretted somewhat at the deprival of her immediate wishes. She sat down at the dining table by the window and looked out wistfully. Then Mercy came back with breakfast and as it was strawberry pancakes, Sundae was much more inclined to enjoy it. Just then Saphire joined Sundae at the table and they had breakfast together. And after they had finished eating, they read together in the gold book of promises. Sundae had such a refreshing feeling afterward, that she became embarrassed at the thought of her earlier attitude.

She confessed this feeling to Saphire, expecting to be reprimanded, but instead Saphire expressed the surprising news that she too had often struggled with the same thing.

"You did?" Sundae exclaimed in disbelief. "But you know the Prince so well that I thought you would never have any problems like that."

Saphire laughed and said, "The changes we must go through are not instantly accomplished. The choices we make each day lead to the long-term effects upon us. That is why we can never look down upon each other when we are all in this process."

Sundae looked gratefully at Saphire, and then spontaneously hugged her. "You are the best sister," she told Saphire. Saphire responded with such a look of blissful satisfaction on her face, though she did not reply. Sundae could see how much this meant to Saphire, and she was very glad she had spoken these words to her.

"Now let's go to the garden," said Saphire, and so they did.

The roses and the lilies were all in bloom, and the fragrance was filling all their senses. In her joy, Sundae began singing the song of the Prince's love for his people, and when she turned around, there he stood at the gate smiling at her.

He came into the garden, and Sundae ran to him and put her arms around him, and he put his arms around her. "This is the best place to be," thought Sundae, and she closed her eyes. "No one else can make me feel the way he does."

The Prince held her in his arms for a few moments, then he took her hand and they walked together through the garden. Saphire lingered behind them, watching and smiling to herself. She remembered how the Prince had walked with her as a child through these same gardens. She still felt as beloved to him as she had then, and she was glad to see that Sundae was now enjoying that same love.

"If only I could rescue many more children," thought Saphire earnestly as she remembered her days of living in the evil kingdom for that purpose. "At least, Pearl has been rescued, and now she has sent Sundae to me."

Roger appeared at the gate just then; his riding lesson was over for the day, and it was his turn to have a meeting with the Prince. Sundae returned to Saphire's company, and they filled watering cans and watered the roses, while Roger walked with the Prince.

Every now and then Saphire glanced at Roger, and saw the contentment he felt in the Prince's presence, and she was very gratified to see it.

I am sorry that I cannot inform you of the entire content of their conversation, but I do know that the Prince was speaking to Roger about his painful relationship with his father. And when the Prince and Roger walked back to Sundae and Saphire, there was an even more peaceful look on Roger's face.

The Prince left the garden, and Sir Guide arrived to take the children on an excursion to the village. They would be participating in a festival, and there would be games, and puppets, and hayrides, and trained dogs performing tricks.

Sundae and Roger, Abel and the other village children became more acquainted with each other and had such a pleasant time. At the end of the day, there was a musical waterworks show with many different colors, and this was the highlight of the festival.

Sir Guide escorted a very tired but happy Sundae and Roger back to the palace.

Chapter 18

In the days following, Roger became much more adept in wielding a sword. He and Abel practiced in the field every day and the sunlight glinted off their blades, flashing back and forth as they thrust and parried. Sir Guide stood watching and smiling his approval, saying nothing unless he had to make some slight correction to their techniques.

Both boys were well on the way to becoming accomplished riders as well, and Roger had no more fear of his horse. He was comfortable in the saddle and at ease with her gait, changing his body stance to adjust to the different rhythms of her movement. He was aware of the changes in her muscular legs as she moved into different gaits, and he was learning how to care for her legs properly with liniment, at the end of the day.

When Roger arrived at the stable early each day, he didn't saddle Starlight right away. Sir Guide advised the boys to spend time with the horses in a non-working way, to observe the horses' personality traits and to allow the horses to bond with them. Roger learned how Starlight preferred to be petted, what treats she liked, and that she responded when he spoke softly and calmly to her. He learned how to brush her coat and how to clean her hooves.

The reward of Starlight's developing trust in him was an exhilarating experience for Roger. Now when he came to the pasture, Starlight had no hesitation in coming to him. It seemed as if his heart jumped when he saw her excitement at his arrival. Roger understood better how fiercely the Prince would protect those who trusted in his care, for now Roger possessed a strong desire to protect Starlight from any harm.

Starlight put her head down when she was near him; this meant she submitted to him. She now trusted him. This rapport with her was so comforting and reassuring to Roger.

Trust is a remarkable thing. As Roger became even more closely acquainted with the Prince, he was so grateful that there could be a person with so much power and authority and yet who was so humble that Roger could absolutely trust in him.

Every promise that Roger read in the gold book affirmed this trust in every possible way or situation. These promises were a guarantee of the Prince's ongoing affection, love, and care for Roger throughout his entire lifetime. It was like a written contract truer than any legal document known; it had been validated and certified by the Prince's own blood.

Sir Guide was now training Abel and Roger to ride while wearing the suit of armor. Although this armor was exceedingly lightweight in comparison to other types of armor, there was some adjustment to the change in attire while riding. Next they would proceed to duel with swords while on horseback.

In the meanwhile, Sundae had a new friend who came to the castle to spend time with her; it was a girl named Zelia who was from the village. Zelia taught Sundae how to swim.

Now when the girls went to the river, they could go deeper and swim underwater, but only with Saphire's supervision.

There was another place in the Kingdom where the river was very deep and expansive, and Zelia's older brother Nate kept a sailboat there. One day he invited his sister Zelia, Sundae, and their chaperone Saphire to go sailing. They went late in the afternoon and saw the sun go down on the water, and sailed back in the moonlight, in a zig-zag fashion.

Sundae was so inspired with her sojourn on the water that she made Roger and Abel desire to go.

Nate didn't need any persuasion to go sailing, and one afternoon soon after the girls' trip, he took Roger and Abel out on the sailboat. They were much impressed with Nate's skill in maneuvering the sailboat, especially when they had to head upstream.

Though the river here was too deep and wide for swimming, sailing on it still had that same effect of calming and relaxing peacefulness. This was a nice break in routine for Roger and Abel, for they were now in the midst of practicing rigorous sword combat on horseback. Every day Sir Guide noted their improvements, and approved their progress.

Some days the Prince came and observed their practice, and every morning, the Prince would commend Roger's accomplishments and encourage him to persevere.

One morning the Prince announced that he had decided it was time to hold a tournament and showcase all the skills the young men of his kingdom had been learning.

It would be a grand day; there were flags, banners, and grandstands for the audience set up on the castle grounds, and all the contestants practiced diligently and heartily for the occasion. The castle kitchen and the village bakery were kept very busy with preparations, for there would be special cakes and pastries made and served to everyone who came.

The day arrived, and it was exciting to see all the booths and regalia and pageantry that accompanied the tests of skill. The rivalry however was light-hearted, and did not lend itself to any unhappy mortification of any contestant, or any severe disappointment or sense of failure. These attitudes were not at all characteristic of such an event in the Kingdom of Grace. Rather, it had the opposite purpose of instilling confidence in the young men who participated. These young men also raised the hopes of those still in training by their example and fortitude.

Cedric's students displayed their archery skills in the arena below the seating area and were admired and applauded. Then his more advanced students did more difficult assignments and received trophies for their efforts.

Next, there were duels in swordsmanship; Roger and Abel had their part in this. The more advanced students fought in armor, and finally there were the few who fought on horseback.

There were a few who were very advanced in horsemanship, but not combat. This included some girls who performed tricks with their horses or had trained them to do complex steps.

Roger watched this with great interest, and noted some things that he thought perhaps Starlight could be persuaded to try later. He had no doubt of her intelligence or abilities.

For the next event, many of the musicians gathered in the arena and began to play and the girls in the Kingdom performed a dance using colorful ribbons, to a song of the Prince.

There were acrobats and stunt performers, after this, as well as a few story mimes. And then it began to grow dark, and the food booths served supper, which consisted of various hot sandwiches. Families sat on blankets spread out on the grass to eat their suppers.

The last event of the day was a breath-taking fireworks display. The brilliant colors illumined the pitch-black sky and cheered the hearts of all in the Kingdom of Grace that night.

Roger and Abel took care of their horses, rubbing them down in their stables, and carefully stored their armor and equipment, and then they parted company for the night. They were tired, but satisfied from all the activities of the day. After all the things for the tournament were taken down and put away, everyone in the Kingdom rested for several days.

The next morning, the Prince met Roger early and told him that he and Abel would do something different today---no sword practice or training of that kind. They could ride their horses just for leisure this week, and he had asked Nate to come and teach them how to swim. So all that week, they worked on swimming techniques in the river behind the castle.

Toward the end of the week, Nate took Abel and Roger in the sailboat to a place in the river where it was deeper and the current was stronger. There was a massive tree growing on the side of the river which had a very long and thick rope tied to a branch that extended over the water. Nate showed Abel and Roger how to swing out over the river, and let go of the rope to plunge into the water, and then to swim back to the side. It was shocking at first to drop into the water with force enough to go under a ways, but Roger swam up to the surface quickly and made it to the side without lagging. They did this a number of times, until they were quite worn out and had to lie down for a while on the wooden dock where the sailboat was tied.

Roger closed his eyes and almost fell asleep; Abel had to shake him because it was time to leave. They climbed aboard the sailboat but this time, there wasn't quite enough wind for tacking, so they all had to use the oars and row back upstream.

That night Roger was so tired that he went to bed right after the evening meal. Then he woke up in the early morning hours before it was light outside. He had showered before the evening meal the night before, so he pulled on his clothes and boots, grabbed his copy of the gold book and went outside. He went down to the gardens, and lit one of the lanterns so that he could read. Just as he began, he looked up and the Prince was walking towards him in the first gleam of morning light that peeked over the horizon.

"Roger," said the Prince as he came to sit by Roger. "I think you are ready for a mission."

"A what?" asked Roger. "I am sending you and Abel on a rescue mission," said the Prince.

Chapter 19

The morning sun was now rising up, stretching its fingers of light over the land until all the dark of night was gone.

Roger sat near the Prince, trying to grasp what the Prince had just said to him.

"Will there be danger on this mission?" he asked the Prince.

"Yes, there will," answered the Prince, much to Roger's dismay.

"Am I that expendable?" questioned Roger, slightly hurt at this knowledge.

"My father sent me on a mission to rescue you," said the Prince. "Now I am sending you."

"But why?" pleaded Roger. He did not want to go anywhere; he was so happy here in this place.

"Roger," said the Prince in his compassionate voice, "There are others who need to know my love besides you. They will not know if I don't send you."

"I don't want to leave you!" Roger protested. "Surely you could send someone else."

The Prince looked at Roger with such love in his eyes. "I will be with you, though you cannot see me with your eyes. You will know my love in an even deeper way, when you share it with others."

Roger saw how much it meant to the Prince, and he decided to submit his will to the Prince's. "Yes, I will go," he said, meaning it with all his heart.

The Prince smiled that radiant smile that was worth everything to Roger. Then the Prince said, "There are two young people in a school far to the west of here, and they are longing for me, though they do not realize it yet. You and Abel are close to their age, and you will be able to go into their school as students."

"Do you know their names?" asked Roger, and then he blushed. "That was a dumb question," he said in embarrassment. "Of course you know their names."

The Prince only smiled kindly at Roger. "Their names are Deonsel and Kamaris."

"One of them is a girl?" Roger asked with some consternation. He was not sure he would know how to relate to a girl besides his sister.

"Don't let that trouble you," said the Prince. "Abel has a sister close in age to himself, and he will know how to be a brother to this girl."

Roger looked relieved when he remembered Rhoda. Girls were not such odd creatures.

The Prince knew what Roger was thinking, and he looked amused. He knew better than anyone that the day would come when one of those "odd creatures" would be very appealing to Roger. It was best that this did not occur yet, for it might interfere with their mission.

"What about Sundae?" asked Roger. "Will she stay here with you?"

"Yes," answered the Prince. "She will be well cared for in your absence. I have asked Rhoda to spend time with her so she will not be missing you so much, and also she has Zelia as a close friend."

This was of great comfort to Roger.

Later that morning, the Prince confided in Sundae about the mission, and Rhoda was with him. From that day on, Rhoda was with Sundae and Saphire very often, to make the separation easier for both Sundae and Roger. Rhoda was a very high-spirited girl, and she would not allow Sundae to remain in a melancholy state. In his wisdom, the Prince had appointed just the right person to help in this situation. Roger perceived this, and admired the Prince's understanding of their needs so much more than even before this day.

Yes, trust is a remarkable thing. It is a necessary ingredient for any adventurous mission, and it had grown in Roger. He was now meek enough to embark on a mission.

As was Abel; he had learned this from his parents. They had trained their children to be available for just such an assignment, and though they were concerned for his safety, they were willing to let him go. Abel had also personally accepted the Prince's request.

Now, Sir Guide would prepare the two boys, who almost could not be called that anymore; they were on the verge of becoming young men.

Sir Guide informed them of the plans: they would go by horseback to this region in the west, and they would be staying with a farmer by the name of Barzillai, who had a stable for their horses. This man would have provisions for them and would treat them kindly, for he knew and respected the Prince.

Abel and Roger were given clothing that was similar to the kind worn in that region, and especially for those attending that particular school; but they were also instructed to bring their armor, and store it at the home of Barzillai. Hopefully, they would not need it. "It is a wise thing never to use a sword unless instructed to do so," said Sir Guide.

They would have cloaks for traveling, and a shoulder bag to carry their most necessary items. These included some tablets to purify the water in this other land so that they could drink from its rivers, canteens for drinking, a flask of oil to heal wounds, a tinder box with which to kindle a fire, and of course, their gold books. Their saddlebags contained food for the journey for their horses and themselves, and some extra clothing.

It was not yet time for them to leave, for the Prince wanted to meet with them individually.

Roger met with the Prince in his garden in the early morning hours of the day before their departure.

The Prince was waiting for him, eager to see him, and spend this time with Roger. "I have so much to tell you," he said to Roger, once Roger was within the garden proper and they had walked a little ways.

Roger looked up at the Prince inquisitively. He realized again that he would never know all there was to know of the Prince, even in a lifetime.

The Prince opened a gold book, and Roger looked into it and saw a mirror.

"Look closely," said the Prince, and Roger focused on the mirror intently. Gradually, he saw an image of the Prince appear in this mirror.

"This is how you can see me, when you are away from my physical presence," said the Prince. "And the more you look at me in this book, the more you will be made like me, and you will understand me better and better."

"When you were still fighting me---do you remember?" asked the Prince.

That night seemed so long ago to Roger now, but he did remember the night he attempted to have a sword battle with the one he knew now as the Prince.

"Do you remember how you asked me for my name, and I said I only give my name to those who surrender to me?" asked the Prince.

Roger nodded; he remembered that now, though he had almost forgotten that part of the night's strange events.

The Prince looked earnestly at Roger and he said: "I can now give you my name; for you are under my authority. My name is Victory and because of your allegiance to me, you now have victory, even when outward circumstances don't look like it. You will have my peace which gives you victory, my love which comforts you, and my joy which strengthens you."

"You will experience these things in an even greater way, because you will have greater need. Remember my promises always! Don't let them depart from your mind," warned the Prince. "The evil prince also has his representatives in that school, and he will attempt to change your mind about me. Remember that he always lies; this is his character."

The Prince held Roger close to himself in an embrace, and then he released him with one more admonition: "There is nothing more powerful than the antidote in my blood, Roger. This is the proof of my love for you---that I shed my blood for you. Never forget it."

Roger looked into the Prince's eyes and saw again that deep kindness that was endless. He flung his arms around the Prince and clung to him, until it was time to leave the garden. Then they slowly walked out together.

Chapter 20

The next day, all their friends gathered to show support of Roger and Abel's mission. Roger and Abel were wearing their armor over their clothing and all their supplies were ready. The horses were saddled and bridled, and stood close by, every now and then showing their excitement by snorting and pawing at the ground. After all, they were warhorses, and they were trained for challenge and adventure.

Sir Guide and the Prince were there to see them off---as well as Saphire, Sundae, Abel's family, Nate and Zelia, and all the rest of the people of the castle. Sir Guide was holding a small bag containing something but Roger and Abel did not know what it was.

Roger nervously and quietly asked Saphire what this was for, and she privately answered that this was used for Sir Guide's benediction. Roger still was not quite sure what that meant, so he kept quiet and waited, for he knew he would soon find out the answer to his query.

He was not long in waiting; Sir Guide announced that he would say the benediction. Sir Guide opened the small bag and took something out that he sprinkled over Roger and Abel with a wave of his hand. It was the golden stuff that was on all the trees in the Kingdom of Grace! "This is my blessing on you," he said. "This represents the prayers of the Prince and his people over you on your mission."

And all of the people standing there held out their right hands to Roger and Abel in a solemn pledge of support for their mission.

Then there were hugs all around; Abel's entire family hugged both of the boys. Then it was Sundae, Saphire, and Mercy's turns; and last the Prince and Sir Guide embraced the boys.

Roger and Abel mounted their horses, and turned the horses' noses towards the west. Then they set out on their journey, looking back one last time and waving goodbye to all who stood there watching as they left. It was a monumental moment in the lives of these two boys.

Saphire stood there watching their departure, and knowing in her heart that when they came back, they would no longer be boys. Then she took Sundae's arm, and Rhoda took Sundae's other arm, and they walked back to the castle where Saphire had something planned for Sundae to take her mind off of the temporary loss of her brother.

The Prince and Sir Guide were the last ones to leave; they stood there talking quietly to each other for some time, before they returned to the castle. I'm sorry that I don't know what they said to each other ----it was a private conversation---- but I'm sure it concerned Roger and Abel's welfare. They knew what Roger and Abel would be facing in the days to come.

As for Roger and Abel, since they had never been there before, they would have to find the intended place in the west through old-fashioned "horse sense" and a map of the region.

Most of all, they would have to depend upon an inner discernment and discretion from their knowledge of the Prince. It is known that people perish from their lack of knowledge, but it is not the lack of academic knowledge that causes demise. It is the lack of knowing wisdom.

Since they both knew the Prince, these boys had access to the source of wisdom. So they set out with confidence in that privilege.

They had studied the map diligently before their departure, and it was carefully stored in Roger's shoulder bag. Sir Guide had given Abel a compass which showed true north. Just now he checked their bearings to make sure they were continuing west.

They had left behind the perimeter of spruce trees surrounding the castle grounds and its small farms and village; now they were riding over wild grasses that waved in the wind. A sea of rolling hills spread out before them, of greens and browns, and dotted with trees here and there. Far in the distance they could see reddish brown mountains covered in white mist.

The sky was gray here, and the daylight seemed grim and unfriendly. Roger was glad for his warm cloak, for the breeze was cold. It made an eerie moaning sound as it meandered through the wild grasses, bending them whichever way it pleased.

They saw no other travelers, and Abel began to sing one of the songs of the Kingdom of Grace. It was a song that reminded them of all the good things the Prince had done, which they cherished. Roger joined in and sang with him; it cheered him to remember these things.

They came to a small grove of trees, and stopped here to have refreshment and to allow their horses to rest. They removed their helmets to eat and drink, but kept their swords strapped to their sides in readiness, though they sincerely hoped they would never have need of them. The horses nuzzled each other as if grateful for the company, and Roger and Abel gave them a small amount of feed. When they would arrive at Barzillai's farm, there would be hay for the horses as well, but they did not know how long it would take to get there.

Just as they finished eating, Abel alerted Roger---they sat very still and listened---there was a slight crunch as if someone had stepped on a twig. Then they caught a fleeting glimpse of movement just beyond where the horses were tied.

The next moment a nymph of a girl stood right in front of them. She was wearing mud-colored leggings, and a greenish-brown tunic that was equally drab. A bow and quiver was slung over her shoulder, and she wore a leather belt with a pouch attached to it. Her skin was the color of an acorn, and her jet-black hair was worn in a long braid down her back. Her eyes were big and dark and unflinching as she stared at Roger and Abel like some woods animal.

"Who are you?" Abel asked her when he could catch his breath again.

"I am your guide," answered the girl. "The Prince sent me to you."

"Do you have a name?" asked Roger.

"Do you?" retorted the girl indignantly.

Roger looked down sheepishly. "I'm sorry," he said to the girl. "I didn't mean any insult."

"My name is Adah," she said in a more kindly tone. "We need to be moving on now."

Roger was a little miffed that their guide was a girl, but after he saw her in action, his disappointment changed to admiration.

Adah made a low, soft sound and a satin-brown horse appeared and stood in the grass just outside the grove. This horse was smaller in stature, and more like a pony; its lower legs, mane and tail were black. It wore a thick pad strapped to its belly instead of a saddle, and instead of stirrups, there were leather loops. Roger quickly saw the reason why there was this difference in equipment for her horse.

Roger and Abel suddenly heard an animal sound that they could not identify. There was something large moving through the waist-high grasses in the field just ahead of them.

Adah sprang into action; at her command (in some other dialect) the horse began to canter. Adah ran and vaulted onto its back, holding on with her knees and notching an arrow at the same time. Her horse stopped suddenly, but the girl did not fall; they heard the twang of her bow and her arrow struck the creature in the grasses. Adah quickly notched another arrow and let it fly, and it hit its mark.

Adah motioned to Abel and Roger to come; they were mounted by now, and slowly and cautiously walked their horses over to Adah. There on the ground was a huge wild boar with tusks; its mouth was open in a vicious expression, but its glassy eyes were now lifeless. Two arrows protruded from its massive form.

"It was a male," explained Adah. "And they are very dangerous."

Roger and Abel said nothing; they simply stared at the monstrous beast that lay on the ground before them. Then Adah turned her horse's head toward the west, and her horse began to walk away. Adah looked behind her to see if Roger and Abel were following.

"We have a ways to go before nightfall," she said. It was humbling in some ways for the boys to follow a girl guide, but after that display of courage, they could say nothing negative. They turned their horses to follow her and headed in the direction she was indicating.

They went for some time through more grassy areas, and the light was becoming grayer; the air felt more damp and colder. Abel checked the compass and noticed that they were veering away slightly from a western course, and he was troubled. Soon, though, he saw the reason for the variance; there was a huge bog on the side of them. In this light, they might not have seen it until it was too late, but Adah knew it was there. If they had fallen into this because of their pride, they would have sunk as if it were quicksand.

Chapter 21

The hills were becoming more steep and craggy
and they could see woods ahead of them. Adah
led the way down into a ravine between the sides
of two hills that were more like small cliffs. The
horses went slowly down the incline and at the
foot of these hills there was a swiftly flowing creek.
The three horses drank thirstily from the creek.
Adah dismounted and filled her canteen and drank
from it before putting it away. Abel and Roger
followed her example; they didn't put any
purification tablets in their water since Adah had
drunk from this stream.

Adah walked alongside the stream, leading her
horse by the reins, until she saw a ravine leading
up through the hills on the other side. The water
was shallow here, and had many flat smooth rocks
in the streambed. Adah beckoned to Roger and
Abel to come, as she said, "We should cross
here."

So they crossed, carefully stepping on the rocks,
and leading their horses through the water. Just
as they were at the water's edge, Roger saw out
of the corner of his eye something black moving in
the water. Starlight reared up, and Roger was
startled and almost fell face down into the water.

He caught his balance and climbed out quickly, still holding the reins. Starlight's front feet came down again and Roger spoke calmly and firmly pulled on the reins. The horse came up the embankment, stomping and shaking her head.

Adah and Abel were already a ways up the slope, and Adah handed her horse's reins to Abel. She went down and put her hands on either side of Starlight's face. She said something in her strange dialect to the horse and this had a calming effect on the horse.

"What was that black thing!" Roger exclaimed in relief that it was behind them, whatever it was. "A water moccasin," answered Adah. "They can be deadly....you handled it well."

Roger was pleased to hear this from someone so experienced in the wilderness. (Even though she was a girl) Then he was too curious to keep from asking her, "What did you tell my horse that calmed her so much?"

"I told her in my language that the Prince is watching over us; that his eye is upon us wherever we go," answered the girl. "You will never be out of reach of his help."

Adah turned and went up the narrow ravine, and Roger followed, leading Starlight. Adah took her horse's reins from Abel and set out on a new path. It was almost dark now and the woods were not far in the distance. They rode their horses as the last bit of sunlight faded away, and then dismounted and led their horses by the reins. They were now at the edge of the woods, and it was dark and foreboding. The boys entered anyway, following Adah as she led her horse, and walking softly as she did.

Once inside, Roger saw that there were shafts of moonlight on a path, and he was not so apprehensive, though the night noises in the woods seemed eerie and menacing to him.

Adah kept going on the path lit by intermittent moonlight, and the boys kept pace with her. There were many tangents leading away in other directions, but Adah kept to the path that seemed to wind and curve its way through the heart of the forest. And then it ended abruptly against a dark cliff face with an even darker recess in the cliff wall. They discovered that this dark recession was the opening to a cave.

Adah told the boys that this was a good place to sleep, but Roger was not so convinced. I don't think he particularly wanted to go into a dark cave without a light, and much less spend the night in that cave with whatever might also be in there!

Adah tied her horse's reins to the closest tree, and Roger and Abel did the same. "Let's make a fire," said Adah, and she began to gather sticks and lay them in a pile a few feet from the front of the cave entrance. Abel and Roger assisted and then Abel used the supplies in his tinder box to start a small flame. Adah had a small clay oil lamp in her supplies, and Abel used the flame to light the lamp, and then put the lighted tinder on the pile of sticks.

Adah gave the lamp to Roger, and he understood that he should explore the cave with this lamp. It wasn't a large amount of light, but by holding the lamp up high, and then down low, Roger could fairly sufficiently check the corners, floor, and ceiling of the small cave. It looked clear of snakes, spiders, and bats, and Roger was grateful.

They ate their supper rations by the firelight, fed and watered the horses, and then Adah took out her bedroll and spread it out just outside the cave entrance by the fire. Roger and Abel looked at each other in surprise; they felt awkward and embarrassed as if they should be offering to sleep outside the cave instead.

"I am used to sleeping outside, and I know the forest," Adah said in response to their disturbed expressions. "I have my bow, and I would prefer to stay closer to the horses and protect them. Please do not trouble yourself on my account."

Roger looked into the cave again, wondering if it would accommodate them all. Adah saw his scrutiny and said, "The cave is small and it would not be right for me to sleep close to a young man to whom I am not married. My life belongs to the Prince."

So Roger and Abel took the clay oil lamp, and spread out their bedrolls in the cave, putting the oil lamp where it could give a little light without being knocked over. Abel fell asleep right away, but Roger stayed awake for a few minutes thinking about Adah's attitude. She had so much respect for herself because of the Prince, and Roger thought this was a very good thing to have. He hoped that Sundae would think of herself that way, too.

Abel woke Roger, and they rolled up their sleeping mats in the early morning light. Adah was up already and had smothered the fire, and was now caring for the horses. She joined Roger and Abel for breakfast, which was Sundae's latest achievement in baking. (Sundae had insisted on packing this sweet bread for their trip.) Adah said she had a younger sister, too, and her name was

Keziah. She also told them that her horse was named Marrona.

Roger wanted to ask her more about her family, but just then Adah took her gold book from her bag and walked away to read by herself. Roger and Abel read in their books also, and then packed up all their supplies and prepared to leave. Abel checked his compass and the map to see where they were. He guessed that it would take one more full day to get there.

They started out again, with Adah leading on her horse. Now there was no more time for conversation, as they traveled single file through the rocky hills and occasionally down into a shallow gully. Then they came into a clearing that was perhaps a valley; the grasses were higher here making it seem like the plains. On the right of this wide expanse was another forested area. They began riding across this clearing toward the mountain range in the distance.

Suddenly, a flock of wild geese rose up and flew swiftly over their heads. Their honking in the distance as they flew away seemed to herald a warning. Then Adah stopped and Roger could tell that she was watching something.

"What is it?" asked Roger.

"I saw a jackrabbit scurrying into its hole," said Adah. "There is a storm coming."

A few seconds after she said this, dark clouds began boiling at the horizon line and then spreading rapidly toward the sky overhead. They saw streaks of jagged lightning flashing off and on in the distance, and then there was a low rumble of thunder.

Adah took all this in, and then she said, "It's going to be a bad one. We must take cover in the forest." She turned her horse's head in that direction, and took off at a gallop. Abel and Roger looked at each other, then prodded their horses into a gallop as well, and rode hard after her.

They made it into the woods just as the storm broke; it was a downpour. Here, the forest was dense enough that they were not drenched, but Adah stayed close to the cliff side, and searched for another cave. She was successful and this one was large enough that even the horses could take shelter in it with them.

When they were safely inside the cave, she said, "It is a lightning storm; it's better to be here than under trees or out in the open."

She was right about that; even here, they could see how often the sky was lit up from jagged bolts of lightning piercing the gray clouds. At least, they were not totally in the dark here, as the cave entrance was wide and the lightning was so frequent.

"If there is lightning in dry heat, it can set a tree on fire. But with all this rain, a fire would be put out," she said, hoping to cheer Roger and Abel. She could see that they were both discouraged. There was nothing to do but wait it out, and this would certainly delay their arrival at the farm. They had no idea how long the storm would last---or if they would run out of food before it did. The thought of staying here at night was not a happy one.

Chapter 22

Roger was definitely discouraged; they were on a mission for the Prince, and yet they ran right into a storm. Why had the Prince allowed this? Had they done anything wrong? He finally asked Abel what he thought about this, but Abel had never been on a mission before either, and he didn't have an answer.

Adah answered them both. She said, "Trouble doesn't mean that you were not obedient, or that you did not follow directions correctly. We will not be able to understand all the ways of the Prince; his ways are far above ours. He is always working things out, though, that will eventually turn into something good."

The storm continued pummeling the earth in its fury, creating furrows of trickling water on the ground and sending rivulets of water cascading over the cliff above this cave. They were cold and wet and hungry by now. The horses were just as miserable. Roger and Abel took the heavy saddles off of them and tried to dry them with the saddle blankets, though these were damp also. They looked out bleakly at the dismal scene of dripping trees; there could be no fire now since all the wood was wet.

Adah spoke up in the silence of their disgruntled demeanor. "We have only two choices," she said. "We can either grumble and complain and think that the Prince no longer cares; or we can trust in him and know that he loves us no matter where we are or what is happening around us."

Abel spoke up as if to remind himself: "He never said it would be easy."

Roger reminded himself of the same thing. "I guess he meant that victory is being able to rejoice even in unpleasant circumstances because of his love for us."

"We quickly forget all that he has done for us or given to us when we are tired and discouraged," said Adah. "There is no power greater than that which is in his blood."

"I forget about that power," said Abel. "I think I have not truly trusted in his promises."

"Maybe what we need is much more than just reading them," said Roger thoughtfully.

"We have only seen the Prince in a form like ours. If we saw him as he is in his father's realm, we would not even be able to look at him. It would be like looking directly at the sun. The Prince humbled himself to be like us, and to die for us.

But we must not forget who he is; his father is the King of the universe and has all authority. The Prince is not like a man who could lie; when he gives us his word he will not break it," said Adah fervently.

So they set their minds to memorizing the promises of the Prince; and all during that stormy weather, they were storing up the treasures of the Prince in their hearts. They walked around the cave reciting to themselves and to each other the Prince's words in the gold books.

When the storm broke, and the sun peeked out cautiously from its hiding place, they felt as strong as lions coming out of their lair.

They saddled their horses once more, loaded up their belongings, and led their horses out of the cave and into the forest. Once out of the forest, they would need to go into the clearing and head west again. Adah led the way back through the woods in the direction they had come. The forest was still terribly wet and muddy, so they walked and led their horses by the reins. It was hard to look ahead to see where they were going and what was in front of them and at the same time, look at their feet and where they were stepping.

Suddenly Roger felt intense pain in his ankle; he glanced down and saw that he had stepped into the vises of a metal animal trap and it had closed on his ankle. He could not move, and the intense pressure made him groan out loud and he was sweating.

Adah and Abel instantly saw what was wrong. They tied the horses to a tree, and began looking for a branch strong enough to pry apart the vises of the trap. After looking in the area just beyond them for a few minutes, Adah suddenly told Abel to take all the horses and get out of the woods, using the compass, and wait in the clearing.

Abel looked at Adah in disbelief until she explained. "Did you see that black lump back there on the ground that looks like it has red berries in it?" she asked. "That is the dung of a black bear, and it was fresh," she said, pulling an arrow from her quiver. "You will be heading away from it, judging by the tracks. Go now before it turns and comes this way."

So Abel heeded what she said, and he led the horses towards the way out of the wood and into the clearing, though he hated the thought of leaving Roger with his foot in a trap.

"Roger," said Adah. "Wake up; don't faint," she pleaded and shook him a little, for he was very pale and listless. Adah notched the arrow to her bow and waited. Her eyes squinted as she watched all around for any sign of movement.

Then she saw it. Now came the hardest part; waiting until the exact moment when she had the most chance of a good shot. If she tried and failed.....she couldn't think of that. She held her arm steady and concentrated on her target, holding her breath, willing herself to wait even though the tension made her feel feverish. Then she knew the moment, and she let the arrow fly----the animal reacted to the impact, snarled and began charging. Quickly she notched another arrow and let it fly. She finally let her breath out when she saw the animal keel over. She didn't go over to it to investigate; instead she stayed by Roger's side and talked quietly to him. "Roger," she said. "I killed the bear. We're going to be alright. The Prince will send us his help to get you out of this trap."

She was right; not long afterward, a man wearing a fur skin vest and hat came walking up to Adah and Roger. "Now that's a shame," he said. "I see you done got yourself tangled up in my little bear trap. I'll be gettin' you out in no time. This here's your friend, Adah?" asked the man, who was a trapper by trade.

"Yes," answered Adah. "I couldn't pry the trap open---I need something metal."

But the man was already working on prying the trap open with the barrel of a gun; he had been carrying a black powder rifle over his shoulder. As he pried the trap open, Adah lifted Roger's foot out of the trap.

"Good thing he had them boots on," said the man. "The injury won't be nearly as bad. Now what you done with my bear?"

"I killed it," said Adah. "It's over there," and she pointed in the direction where the bear was lying.

"Adah, you done me proud! I shore didn't know you could shoot a bear," said the man.

"I did what I had to," said Adah, pulling off Roger's boot as he grimaced. She looked at his ankle; it was badly bruised, but Adah was thankful to see that there were no puncture wounds from the sharp points on the trap.

"Do you have any extra gun powder?" Roger asked the man in a very faint tired voice, as Adah helped him put the boot back on his injured foot.

"What you got to trade for it, son?" asked the man, pulling a small leather bag from his larger bag of belongings.

Roger looked dismayed; he didn't know if he could part with any of his supplies. Adah turned around and took something out of the pouch on her belt. "Would you take salt?" she asked.

"Salt! Why, shore, I would. That's as good as gold," said the man, and he made the trade with Adah for the black gunpowder. "Well, I best be going---I got a bear to skin." He held out his hand to Roger and helped him up on his feet, nodded to him and then he turned and walked away.

Adah put Roger's arm over her shoulder, and helped him limp his way out of the woods.

Abel was waiting in the clearing with the horses, and his tense face muscles relaxed into a relieved smile when he saw Adah and Roger coming out of the woods. Abel took over and helped Roger get up on his horse.

After Adah mounted, she turned to ask Roger something: "What did you want that gunpowder for? There are not many guns like that around here."

Roger answered her that he just had a feeling that it might be of some use to them. Adah didn't question him anymore; she didn't know much about guns. She told Abel about the bear, and how the trapper came and pried the trap open.

They were all thankful that the trapper had his gun; they didn't know what else could have been used to open the trap. So with grateful hearts, they turned towards the west and headed across the clearing.   Adah hoped they could find shelter under the rocky cliffs beyond the clearing before nightfall.

Chapter 23

They rode through the clearing without any mishap, and the sun was shining, although the light felt colder here than before. The wind blew through the grasses in a melancholy way in the late afternoon sun, and the shadows playing on a few large rocks here and there were becoming darker.

The cliffs ahead were a reddish color, and the sun began to go down behind them in streaks of orange and blue, striped with yellow. The sun looked like a white ball of fire as it slowly sank below the ridge.

It was almost dark when they reached the cliff ridge. Adah cautioned about snakes as she and Abel dismounted and led their horses up a steep incline between two ridges. There was the dark entrance of a cave in the rock wall; it was very tall which usually meant it would be a large cave. Roger watched from below; he would have to wait until they came back and helped him. Adah and Abel were on the way down now and looking on the way for firewood.

The only thing growing here was short stubby trees and small bushes. "That sword might be useful now," said Adah, motioning towards the short trees. "Those tree limbs look dry."

So after they helped Roger up the slope to the cave, Abel took his sword and chopped off some limbs from these short trees, until he had an armful. These he brought back up to the cave. They made a fire just inside the entrance, since they could not see into the deep recesses of the cave. Once the fire was going, they hoped to see better into the cave.

Adah's clay lamp was far too small a light to see further back into the cave, but Adah lit it anyway to get a closer look at Roger's foot. She pulled his boot off as carefully as she could and examined his foot. "It's swelling," she said. "We will need to elevate it."

Abel and Adah brought all the horses into the cave, though they kept close to the opening. Abel took the saddles off and used one of the saddles to prop Roger's foot up.

"I have some herb medicine to make a poultice," Adah said. She took a small package of dried plants and a small mortar and pestle from her bag. After she crushed the plants very finely, she poured a small amount of oil into the bowl and made a paste. Then she rubbed this mixture on Roger's ankle. She rummaged in her supplies and found a long strip of cloth which she wound tightly around Roger's ankle and then tied.

Roger stayed in this position throughout the night, except when he sat up to eat with Adah and Abel, or when he had to hobble outside to relieve himself.

Abel helped him, and then left him for a few minutes to give him some privacy. Roger looked up at the stars twinkling white in a black velvet sky and sighed. It was the worst of times to have a severely bruised ankle, for he knew that normally it would not heal quickly.

"I wish that I could talk to you right now," Roger said softly, looking up at the stars. "I need your help." He felt sure that the Prince would have a solution for this ankle problem. He remembered how the pain in his arm went away in an instant when he was with the Prince.

Abel came outside and helped Roger back into the cave, and Roger returned to his place with his foot up on the saddle. Adah gave him some medicine to help the pain and allow him to sleep, and it worked. Her pallet was by the horses, away from the boys, and she lay down.

Adah didn't fall asleep right away; she lay there listening. She heard something; at first, she could not identify the sound—then she realized what it was. It was the scream of a mountain cougar, and she was very glad they had brought the horses in with them into the cave.

Abel heard it, too, and sat up. "What is that?" he whispered to Adah, coming closer to her so he didn't wake Roger. "It sounds like a woman screaming."

Adah whispered back, "It isn't. It's a cougar---a mountain lion."

Abel sighed. "Well, at least there are no birds of prey around here."

Adah quietly replied, "Don't be too sure of that. I will stay with you as long as needed since I have a bow."

Abel went back to his place, and then they both settled down to sleep.

At dawn, Abel and Adah were wakened by a whooshing sound and many squeaking noises. A colony of bats was returning to the cave where they would spend the daytime hours hanging upside down in the darkest places of the cave.

That was not so alarming, but what they saw in the front of the entrance was very disturbing. A large snake had coiled itself in the entrance way to bask in the warmth of the sunrise.

Adah and Abel could not agree on what should be done. Adah didn't think Abel could get close enough to use the sword without getting bitten, and Abel didn't want Adah to use the few arrows she had left. They couldn't get close enough to crush it with a stone either; it was the venomous type of snake that could strike quickly. If they threw smaller rocks at it, this would only aggravate the snake into aggression.

In the end, it was Marrona who had the solution. Adah noticed how the horse was blowing and acting excited. After waking Roger and helping him to move out of the pathway, Adah untied Marrona. Marrona moved quickly and stomped the snake from behind before it could raise its head up and strike. The horse stomped the snake until it was lying in several pieces in the cave entrance. As he watched this, the back of Roger's neck tingled with the shock of fear, and his mouth hung open.

Adah went closer to Marrona, who was trembling and snorting after the ordeal. Adah talked soothingly to her horse and praised the mare for killing the snake. The horse put her nose close to

Adah's face in an affectionate manner, and Adah rubbed her horse's face.

Abel went to look at the head of the snake, but Adah warned him not to touch it. "It can still bite and poison you, even up to an hour afterward," she said.

So Abel carefully picked up each piece of the snake's body with his sword and threw them several yards away from the entrance of the cave.

Roger was still in disbelief. "How did you know your horse could do that without getting bitten?" he asked Adah.

"I didn't know," said Adah. "I just trusted the horse's instincts, and apparently she knew what to do. Maybe she had seen other horses do this."

After Marrona was sufficiently calmed down, and all the horses had water and feed, Adah prepared to look at Roger's ankle. Since there was swelling, she had not put the boot back on his foot, so that all she had to do now was remove the cloth wrapped around his ankle.

She fully expected to see an even darker color in his bruised ankle, but instead the color was almost normal. She gently turned his foot, rotating it in different directions, and each time asked how it felt. Roger was as surprised as she was that there was very little pain at all.

"Well, let's see how it feels to walk on it," Adah said, as she slid Roger's boot back onto his foot. Abel helped Roger stand, and then Roger cautiously took a step on the injured foot.

His face registered the surprise he felt at the lack of pain. Adah's face broke into a huge smile, and she said reverently, "The Prince has power to heal those who trust in him."

Roger was ecstatic. He exclaimed: "He heard me! I asked him last night for his help with this problem, and he heard me and answered me."

Adah smiled and said softly, "He can hear you wherever you go. You are never out of his sight."

Abel took his gold book out of his bag and opened it. For a minute, he saw the Prince's face on the page, instead of the printed words. He was so happy that he urged Roger and Adah to take their gold books out, too, and examine them.

Roger did and saw the same phenomenon that had amazed Abel. For a few minutes, he saw the face of the Prince in the book as if it were a mirror. Then he remembered what the Prince had told him before they left on this mission.

Adah too saw the Prince's face in the gold book that morning, and it cheered and encouraged her, too. "You know what this means, don't you?" she asked the boys. "It means that when we read the Prince's promises to us, we will see what he is truly like."

So before they ate their morning meal, they read the promises of the Prince, and the sunlight beaming into the entrance of the cave felt like the light of the Prince warming their hearts. Then they ate together, and prepared to leave the cave.

Chapter 24

In the early morning light, they led their horses
down the steep slope between the cliff ridges.
Roger's ankle was completely healed, and he was
grateful to be able to walk without any hindrances.
In his heart, he told the Prince thank you over and
over again.

When the sun rose up fully, it was hot on the red
rock of these cliffs. Their path was so uneven and
so up-and-down, that they did not mount their
horses here at all. Their horses' hooves made a
loud clop on the hard rocky surfaces, and the sun
beat in their faces.

At noon they looked for a shady spot in the cliff
ridge to rest and refresh their selves and the
horses. They found a place where one jutting
ridge shadowed another, leaving a space of shade
in between the ridges. So they stopped here and
ate, and gave the horses water.

When they began their journey again, they came
to two ridges which were almost joined together at
the top, and there was a narrow passageway
between this, which led down. Adah led the way
through this; it was so narrow that they had to walk
single file. When they got to the end of this trail, it

opened up into a valley. Beyond the valley was a brown mountain range.

They were close now to their destination; the farmer's ranch was in this valley, and the school was in a town at the base of those brown mountains.

It was windy here in this valley and there was more vegetation, though there were still some large flat red rocks here and there. There were several wooded areas in the distance, but they would have to cross this large open place before reaching any woods.

The ground was level here, so they rode their horses, heading west according to Abel's compass and Adah's sense of direction. They were still cautious about snakes in this area, and looked carefully as they walked their horses. Suddenly Adah stopped and took her bow off her shoulder and pulled an arrow from her quiver.

A huge dark shadow came over them and they heard the scream of a bird of prey. "Stand still!" Adah commanded her companions, and they stopped in their tracks. She turned her horse around and faced her friends as the bird circled and came back over them. As it drew near and was almost over Roger and Abel, she had a clear view of the bird's underside, and she let the arrow fly. The arrow penetrated the bird's underside, causing it to scream in pain and turn in an arc. Then it circled to come back in its fury and pursue its attack.

Adah was ready with a second arrow. "Don't move," she yelled to the boys. They were the bait, so they had to stay where they were. This time the bird was flying even lower and screaming with a terrible screech. Roger and Abel could barely stand the noise, and the horses wanted to bolt, but they obeyed their masters and stood still. Even in his terror, the thought struck Roger that this is what it meant to be meek.

Adah took aim when the bird was almost over the boys, and the arrow pierced the bird's throat. The bird tried to fly high again, but it only managed to fly away a short distance before its wings bent and it collapsed, falling to the ground.

They had to take a little while to calm the horses, (and their selves) after this frightening occurrence, and then they proceeded to head west again across the valley.

They made it across without any more trouble, and arrived at the farmer's house in the early evening. Barzillai was in a pasture by his home, and saw them approaching. He went into his home for a few moments, then came outside and waited for them.

"Greetings!" Barzillai said warmly as the boys rode up to his pasture. "Let me show you the stable." He led the way to the stable while the boys and Adah dismounted and followed him.

The stable was large and roomy and had a loft filled with hay. There were at least a dozen stalls, and half of these were empty. Barzillai and his groomsman showed Roger, Abel, and Adah where to put their horses. The saddles were removed and the bridles hung, and each horse was brushed and given hay and water. The boys' armor and weaponry was carefully stored in a tack room in the stable where it would be out of sight but easily accessible.

Then Barzillai led the way back to his house. His wife greeted them at the door, and invited them all to come in for the evening meal. She filled a washbasin with fresh water and gave them soap and towels to wash their faces and hands.

They all sat down to eat at a large wooden table underneath a hanging lantern. After they had eaten, Barzillai formally introduced his wife Salome and his groomsman Tobias, and the two shepherds, Uriel and Malachi, who came in from the fields to eat with them. Barzillai was more of a rancher than a farmer, the boys realized as he told them about himself. Roger and Abel introduced themselves to everyone, and then Adah introduced herself as one of the people of the Book. Barzillai smiled with recognition and told Adah that he knew of her people and their bravery. Adah thanked him graciously for his kindness and hospitality.

"Now then," Barzillai said, "We must discuss the plans. I understand that you boys will be entering the local school as new students. This will not be unusual for there are many transient workers because of the mining industry. Adah, of course, will not be able to pose as a student, because her people are too well known. They have a reputation for their faith in the Prince and his words."

Adah nodded in agreement and Roger and Abel listened carefully. "I think it best that you use your own names, since you are not known here, and that way you will not forget or slip and say the wrong name," said Barzillai. "All that you need say, if you should be questioned, is that you are staying with a family friend. Adah, what are your plans?"

Adah looked up and said, "I am here as a guide; I don't have any further directions. But I think they will need my help on the return trip, so I feel I should stay close by until they are ready to return home, although I do not know how long that might take."

Barzillai's wife spoke up then. "You are welcome to stay here as long as you like," she said.

"Thank you," answered Adah. "But I will not stay as your guest without working on your farm. Is there anything that I could do to be of benefit to you?"

Barzillai said, "I noticed your skill with the horses, and I know your people have highly trained horses. I would be honored if you would assist Tobias with my horses."

Adah smiled. "I would be delighted," she said.

Then Salome stood, and said she would show Adah where she could stay; it was a small guest room on the side of the kitchen. So Adah followed her out of the room.

Barzillai stood and said that there was room for the boys out in the barracks by the stable, and he led Roger and Abel in that direction, accompanied by Tobias.

There were six bunks in this room; Tobias, Uriel and Malachi all slept out here, which left three empty bunks. At least, Roger and Abel thought so, until there was a scratch at the door, and Uriel let in a large sheep dog that promptly jumped up on one of the bunks. So now it was obvious which ones were for Roger and Abel.

Tobias showed the boys where the clean bedding was kept, and they made up their beds. There was a large washtub in a sort of lean-to out in the back of this building, and a well close by, but it was late so there was not enough light to attempt bathing outside tonight.

The sheep pen was also close by; if there was any hint of danger to the sheep, the sheep dog could be let out immediately to investigate and sound the alarm by barking. Her name was Sheba, and she looked like a cross between a Huskie and a Collie. She lay down now on the bunk, with her front paws crossed over each other and her head on her paws.

There was not a sound from any creatures outside that night, except for the hoots of an owl in a nearby tree. Roger and Abel slept soundly; they were very grateful to sleep in a room since they had slept in caves the last few nights.

Just before he fell asleep, Roger looked out of the small windows just under the roof line. He could see the stars, and this was a comfort to him. He thought of the Prince, and he missed him, but at the same time he felt somehow that the Prince was not far away.

In the morning, when the first rays of light streamed through the windows, Roger took out his gold book and read of the promises, and he saw the face of the Prince on the page, smiling at him. "The Prince's kindness shows through his words," Roger thought to himself. And then it was time to get up; breakfast here was served early for the sake of the farm workers. Tobias, Uriel, and Malachi had gotten up before it was light and gone about their duties. Then they would take a break and eat breakfast at the main house.

Abel and Roger bathed and dressed and joined the others for breakfast. They were excited and nervous, as they had no idea of what awaited them at the school by the mountain.

Chapter 25

The school building reminded Roger of the faded antique photos of schoolhouses in the "Old West"---during the time of westward expansion when a large part of the North American continent was still only territory and not part of a nation. The one-room building was made of unpainted wood and was set apart from the town's row of buildings. This room was equipped with a large pot-belly stove for heat; the pipe for this extended through the ceiling and out of the roof for ventilation.

At least the room was not as small as some that Roger had seen in pictures; this one could accommodate four rows of six wooden tables, which could each seat two students. One side of the room was for younger students and these tables were smaller; the other side was for the older children.

There was a blackboard across the front of the classroom, and the teacher's desk was positioned in the front on the right side of the room. Down the length of the long walls were shelves for storing one's personal belongings, with pegs beneath them to hang jackets.

Roger and Abel had walked to the school from Barzillai's ranch, and had made it here just in time, since they did not know how long it would take. The teacher was ushering in the students just now, and Roger and Abel stood in the back of the line and waited.

The teacher was a thin man who looked to be in his thirties, and he looked curiously at the two new faces in the line. "Who are you, and are you planning to be here for very long?"

Roger and Abel introduced their selves, but couldn't give an accurate answer for the second question, so they replied that they were not sure of the length of their time here.

"Well," said the teacher, "You must know that you will not receive a certificate for advancement unless you can fulfill the quota of days present. I won't tolerate slackers. So if you don't want to learn, you will not be allowed to stay."

The boys assured the teacher that they would do their best to fulfill this, and that they did want to learn.

The teacher allowed them to go in, and Roger and Abel looked around for a vacant table. The last table in the row by the wall was empty, so they went and sat at this table.

Roger and Abel both felt a little thrill of excitement when the teacher called the names of two students, Deonsel and Kamaris, and asked them to pass out the books to the older students.

It was a very strange feeling to be in a school with many different ages and levels of education, but it was also very interesting to Roger. He was fascinated with the science book, as it was mostly on geology and rocks and mining, with some chapters about plants and their specific medicinal qualities.

There was a text book on architecture, and Roger looked at this curiously; this was somewhat of a history book. One chapter explored the development of plumbing and the evolution of the "garderobe" into the "water closet". Roger understood from the pictures that these were the precursors of the modern toilet, but the book did not mention that.

It seemed that he had gone back in time when he placed his hand on the mirror in the antique shop. But perhaps he could learn something from looking back at the past; at least, he could learn appreciation for the present time when he would return.

That thought jolted him; he wasn't sure if he ever wanted to return to his own world. He wondered if the Prince would allow him to stay….and if his mother would be allowed to come.

Just then, he realized he had wandered away in thought, and the teacher had noticed. Quickly he regained focus on the subject at hand, which was algebra. He was not delinquent in that subject at home, and this proved to be the same as in his time period.

Spelling was typically a challenge for him, and he encountered the same thing even here, as he struggled to memorize how to spell words like ubiquitous and cacophony. At that point, he was slightly envious of Adah working in the stable at Barzillai's ranch.

At lunch break, Abel and Roger were able to meet the two students, Deonsel and Kamaris. Barzillai's wife Salome had been so kind to pack a lunch for the boys, and they sat outside on a log to eat. Deonsel had a more openly friendly personality, while Kamaris was shy, but upon invitation, they both came to sit on the log with Abel and Roger.

All that week, Roger and Abel met with Deonsel and Kamaris at lunch time, and slowly developed a friendship with them. Roger and Abel instinctively felt that at the appropriate time, they would know how to speak of the Prince. So they said nothing at first; they didn't want to alarm their new friends who might not have the right idea about the Prince. If they could encourage Deonsel and Kamaris to trust their friendship, Roger was sure that then the new friends would be more likely to listen when he and Abel spoke about the Prince.

So they waited, and hoped, and in the meantime they searched for things to talk about that would not reveal their true identity. Roger smiled to himself at the thought of being like a "secret agent" for the Prince.

Finally, the day came, and Roger felt that the Prince was very close to him that day, as he began to tell Deonsel and Kamaris about the Prince. They listened intently, and almost eagerly, until the teacher rang the bell which meant that the lunch break was over.

The next day was the same; the four friends met at lunch break and Roger and Abel answered many questions that Deonsel and Kamaris had about the Prince. It seemed to Roger that the hearts of their new friends were being won over to the Prince. Yet, how would they meet him, Roger wondered; would they need to make the dangerous journey back to the Kingdom of Grace? How would this be possible? Then Roger was ashamed for wondering how something might be possible for the Prince. Everything was possible with the Prince.

They would just have to trust in the Prince for his direction.

The next day Roger and Abel brought their gold books to show to Deonsel and Kamaris. They felt perhaps the Prince might reveal himself through his promises to these two students who were longing to know him. At lunch break, they were careful to be discreet about the books, and made sure that no one was close by when they showed them to Deonsel and Kamaris, who were both very interested to read in the gold books.

Then the trouble began. After lunch break, the teacher made a terrible announcement in front of all the students. "I have been informed that someone has brought a forbidden item to the school grounds," said the teacher. "This will not be tolerated. If it should happen again, those items will be confiscated. You are forbidden to speak of anything in those books ever again at this school, or you will be dismissed. Do I make myself clear?"

Roger and Abel tried to look straight ahead and not at each other, and to keep their expressions from revealing their dismay. Roger's immediate concern was his desire to know who had spied on them and reported it to the teacher.

Now the other students treated Roger and Abel as if they had the plague and nervously kept away from them. One boy looked at them mockingly and Roger was sure he was the one who had spied on them maliciously. After school was over, Deonsel furtively told Abel that he didn't think he and Kamaris would be able to talk with them anymore. Then Deonsel quickly walked away from Roger and Abel, without looking back.

Roger and Abel walked back to the ranch in great disappointment. They were extremely discouraged, and wondered why they had to travel all this way and go through all those difficulties if it was only going to end up like this. Then Abel realized that they were falling into despair instead of trusting in the Prince.

As they came to a wooded area that they went through every day, Roger and Abel thought they heard what sounded like a low whistle. Suddenly, they caught sight of Deonsel and Kamaris in the woods. They signaled to Roger and Abel to be silent, and then Deonsel and Kamaris quietly caught up with them.

Deonsel said, "I had to pretend back there at the school, that I wasn't going to have anything to do with you anymore, but I want the truth. If this Prince is the truth, then I want to know him. And I'm not going to let cowards stand in my way."

Kamaris nodded in agreement. "I feel the same way," she said. "We have waited so long to find out about the Prince, because no one is allowed to talk about it."

Deonsel said, "We can come here every day and you can tell us about the Prince. I am not sure if you should keep coming to school. Now that they know about the gold books, they will be watching you." Kamaris agreed, and added in a very serious tone, "People disappear when the authorities get suspicious about them. And we don't know what happens to them."

Chapter 26

Barzillai agreed that Roger and Abel should not go back to the school, after they told him what had happened that day; they could help out around the ranch until the appointed time to meet with Deonsel and Kamaris in the woods.

Uriel and Malachi were grateful to have extra help, because it was time to shear the sheep. That was quite a new experience for Roger, and even for Abel, but neither of them minded it at all. When they were not helping with the sheep, they helped in the stables, and one day they were able to observe the birth of a new foal. They were surprised at its size at birth; they laughed at its long gangly legs, and how wobbly the foal was as it stood up on them.

And each day, they met with Deonsel and Kamaris in the woods as planned. Three days went by without incident; Deonsel and Kamaris read in the gold books avidly and with great interest. They had many more questions, which Roger and Abel gladly answered.

Yet on the fourth day, they did not come to the meeting place, and Roger and Abel were greatly concerned. The boys waited in the woods for several hours, before deciding that they should go back to the ranch.

It was a sad meeting that night at the evening meal, for Roger and Abel were not able to shake off the feeling that something was seriously wrong. Barzillai could not advise them in this situation; all he could say was that they must ask for direction from the Prince.

The next day, Roger and Abel were in the pasture with the sheep when the shepherds realized that one of the older lambs was missing. Malachi stayed with the sheep, and Uriel went to look for the missing lamb. Five hours went by before Uriel returned with the lamb on his shoulders. Everyone was greatly relieved to see Uriel's success, and he smiled gratefully, but kept on walking to the barn where he would care for the wandering lamb.

Roger and Abel were reluctant to leave Malachi alone with all the other sheep, but it was getting close to the time that they had been meeting Deonsel and Kamaris. They felt they should go back and see what would happen, just in case their friends might come. Malachi assured them that it would be all right, so they set out to go to the appointed meeting place.

On the way, Roger confided in Abel that during the incident of the lost lamb, he began to have the thought that perhaps the Prince was urging them to go and look for Deonsel and Kamaris, as if they too were lost lambs.

"This is so strange," said Abel. "I had the same thought, and it became stronger as if it were being impressed on my mind."

"This must be how the Prince is guiding us," said Roger. "If our friends do not come to the meeting place, then I think we should go and look for them."

Roger and Abel waited for several hours, but their friends did not come. Roger wanted to go and look for them immediately, but Abel said no, they should inform Barzillai of their plans. "We may need his counsel, also," said Abel. So the two boys headed back to the ranch.

Barzillai listened intently as the boys described how they both felt the Prince intended them to look for their missing friends. "I am glad you came back to tell me where you are going. I think you should waste no time in going to look for them, even though it is almost night time. Now tell me, what do you know about these friends?"

Roger and Abel did not know a lot about them, except that Deonsel's father was some kind of accountant for the mining business and his mother was a seamstress. Kamaris had no father and her mother worked at the town's only hotel establishment.

"Well," said Barzillai, "Then you should first look in town because it is likely that they live there. Go on your horses and come back here tonight. If you don't find out anything, then in the morning you can begin a search in earnest."

The boys saddled up Starlight and Sunrise and packed a few provisions which Simone gave them, and then they rode away in the direction of the town. They passed by the schoolhouse that was dark and vacant now that school was dismissed for the day. They rode on into the town and came to the hotel, which was more like a large two-story house. Here they dismounted and tied the reins of their horses to the hitching pole, and went to the front entrance and tapped on the oval glass window of the door. There was a large wooden veranda, and they stood there nervously waiting, wondering what they would say. It was a great relief when a woman finally came to the door. She cautiously opened the door.

"Can I help you?" the woman asked, and the boys hesitated for a moment, and then Roger replied. "Ma'am," he said, "We are looking for a classmate of ours---Kamaris. Are you her mother?"

"Why do you want to know?" the woman asked nervously.

"May we come in and speak with you?" asked Abel politely and respectfully.

The woman nodded her head, opened the door, and allowed the boys to come in. "Come in the kitchen with me," she said. "We can speak more privately."

The boys followed the woman into the kitchen in the back of the house. As soon as they were all in that room, the woman asked: "Now tell me what is going on. Kamaris did not come home from school two days ago, and I have not seen her since."

The two boys looked at each other sadly; then Roger said, "We wish we could tell you, but we don't know either. We just sensed that something was wrong and we wanted to find out if that was true or just a feeling."

"What about her friend Deonsel? Do you know if he is missing too?" asked Abel.

"I don't know. Even if I did, that would be none of my business," said the woman. "I've had enough to worry about since Kamaris didn't come home."

"Excuse my ignorance of how things are handled here, but did you report this to the authorities?" asked Roger.

"Humph!" said the woman indignantly. "They are the ones responsible for this!"

"Do you know of any reason that would have made the authorities suspicious of her?" asked Abel.

"Well….she did mention something rather odd….she said she met some people who said the Prince of Grace was a real person," said the woman thoughtfully. Suddenly, she looked startled, and then with a realization showing in her face, she said vehemently: "It was you!! You are the ones who brought this evil!! Get out of my house!!"

"But, wait…we just want to help find her," pleaded Roger.   "Don't you want to find your daughter?"

With an angry look the woman answered, "She's not my daughter! She's my sister's child, and if the authorities have her in custody, there's nothing

I can do about it. Now just leave before I have you arrested for trespassing!"

"You are the only mother she has," said Abel sadly. "Surely there is something you can do..."

"Get out!" the woman said ferociously. "This is your fault, not mine. You should not have come here with those evil lies."

The woman grabbed Roger and Abel by the arms and practically dragged them to the entrance. Letting go of their arms, she quickly opened the door and shoved the boys out. They stumbled onto the porch, and then catching their balance, they untied their horses and led them down the street.

They passed a number of shops and establishments and finally they saw an accounting firm. "This must be Deonsel's father's business," said Abel. "I didn't see any other accounting places."

So the boys tied their horses' reins to the post and went to the door and knocked. A man wearing loose brown trousers and a tweed jacket opened the door. "Yes?" said the man.

"Sir, we are looking for a friend named Deonsel," said Roger. "We thought this might be where he lives."

The man looked up and down the street which seemed deserted by now except for the tavern at the far end of the street. Then he invited the boys to come in, and since he did not seem quite as unfriendly as the last person they encountered, they went in without much hesitation. As soon as the door closed however, the man's countenance became very serious.

Chapter 27

"I am Deonsel's father," said the man. "He has been missing for two days. No one knows what happened to him---or if they do, they are not telling me."

"We would like to help find him, if you would allow us to," said Roger.

"Are you students from his school?" asked the man.

"Yes," said Abel. "We just started going to the school here, and we met him there."

"These are dark times," said the man. "Are you sure you want to get involved with this?"

"Yes, sir, we are," said the boys. "We can start searching tomorrow morning."

"Let's go into my office," said the man. "You can call me Merlono---that is our surname."

Demas Merlono lit a candle in his darkened office, and the boys sat down in chairs opposite the desk behind which Merlono sat down.

"What did you mean by dark times?" asked Roger.

Merlono sighed and rubbed his forehead. "People disappear without a trace, and no one seems to know anything about it....and now it is my son...." His voice began to crack, and faded off, as he suppressed his emotion.

"Did he say anything unusual before his disappearance?" Abel wanted to know.

Merlono paused, and then lowered his voice and said, "He spoke of the Prince of Grace. I warned him not to say anything more about it, because it's against the law here."

"Have you heard of the Prince of Grace?" asked Roger carefully.

Merlono looked hesitant to answer, but then he gave a slight nod. "But it was years ago," he admitted. "I was only a child. After I came here and started a business, I had to put that behind me in order to develop a successful business."

Roger looked at Abel, but said nothing. He felt at that moment as if the Prince was showing him that Deonsel and Kamaris were not the only lost sheep in this town.

"Do you have any idea where we should begin looking?" asked Abel.

"I do have one idea," said Merlono. "I know you will probably think that I am a coward, or that I don't love my son, but it would be best if you go alone. If I close my shop, it will alert the authorities, and end the search altogether. I was at a loss before you came---I did not know what to do; you see I am sure that those in power are responsible for the missing people. I had no one to turn to for help; my neighbors are too afraid to say anything or do anything."

"What is your idea?" asked Roger.

"The old deserted mines," said Merlono. "The trick would be to find them---the entrances have been hidden for years."

"Who would be able to show us?" Abel wondered.

"You might find the answer at the Three Coins Tavern. When people are drunk, they have loose lips, if you know what I mean," answered Merlono. "You should go now...but be on your guard. If you arouse suspicion, you will be in danger also."

The two boys left Merlono's residence, and went down the street to the tavern. The horses were skittish and did not like the sounds coming from the tavern, so the boys tied them to a hitching post nearby, but not in front of the tavern. Roger couldn't blame the horses; he didn't like the sound of it either, and dreaded having to go in this place.

Then he and Abel mustered their courage and went inside. At first the drunken men and rowdy customers didn't pay any attention to them at all; Roger supposed they must be used to curious boys or boys who needed to make some money by sweeping the floors.

As soon as he thought of it, Roger realized that might give them more time to find out something. He quietly mentioned it to Abel, and so they approached the bartender to ask. The bartender looked at them quizzically over the counter, while he was drying a glass and then nodded. "Brooms are over there," he said, pointing to a corner at the end of the long wooden counter. Two brooms were leaning against the wall by a wooden hat-rack there. "Don't disturb the customers," the bartender told them gruffly.

The two boys began sweeping the unoccupied side of the long room, trying to observe everything at the same time. There was a gypsy dancer on the stage, dancing to the music of a cimbalom, as the musician swiftly hammered its steel strings with two metal beaters. At one table, men were playing a game of cards, and at another table a solitary man sat drinking alone. At yet another table a group of men were drinking and laughing and there was a woman with them obviously flirting and pretending to be coy.

This sight sickened Roger; he thought of his own father sitting in bars and wondered how many times his father had been in similar situations. He quickly dismissed that thought, for it would only distract him with grief and he needed to remember why he was here.

The dance ended, and the musician packed up his instrument, and he and the dancer walked across the room and up the stairs. Roger looked up at the stairs and gave a slight nod to Abel. They couldn't do any more sweeping downstairs without coming too close to the customers, so Roger reasoned it would be a good excuse to go and sweep upstairs.

So the two boys quietly went up the stairs, carrying the brooms. When they got to the landing and the inner hallway of the upstairs, they saw the dancer and the musician going to a room. Abel led the way and followed them to their room. He knocked lightly on their door.

The young woman opened the door a crack and peered outside it; her expression was that of surprise when she saw the two boys. "Who are you and what do you want?" she asked quietly.

From within the room, the boys heard the voice of the musician, but they did not understand the language he was speaking.

"We just want to ask a few questions," said Abel. "We're new here."

The dancer answered the musician in their language, and then came out into the hall. "What do you want to know, and why do you ask me, a performer?" she said.

"We thought you would hear a lot of conversations that go on, and we wondered if people ever talk about the deserted mines," said Roger.

The young woman looked sharply at Roger and again at Abel, then she abruptly told them to come in, as she turned and went back into the room.

"Why are you so interested in the deserted mines?" she demanded to know.

"We just heard about them, and it sounds so mysterious that no one even knows how to get into them---we just would like to see them," said Roger.

"You expect me to believe that when you are here so late at a tavern? You expect me to believe you are just curious?" she exclaimed.

"I suppose not," said Abel. "We do have a good reason to find the deserted mines."

"If your reason is good enough, we can take you there," said the woman.

Roger started to speak, but Abel stopped him. "How much money is a good enough reason?" he asked.

"We can do it for five gold pieces," she told him.

"Can you show it to us tomorrow?" asked Abel.

"If you have the gold pieces," she answered.

"All right," said Abel. "We will see you then. What are your names?"

"Tamarina and Tresephen," said the gypsy dancer. "He is my husband."

"Does he speak our language?" asked Roger.

"Not very well," was the reply. "We are from the land across the sea."

"What sea?" wondered Roger.

"The one just beyond this mountain range," said Tamarina. "I must caution you: do not let anyone else know what we spoke of tonight. No one is allowed to go to the deserted mines."

Chapter 28

The boys quickly swept the upstairs hallway, and then came back down the stairs. There were still customers at the tables, so they would not be able to sweep that side of the room. They quietly put the brooms away, and as they did this, the bartender informed them that there would be no payment until the job was complete. They assured him that they would come back in the morning and finish when the room was empty.

This would also give them an excuse for coming back to meet with Tamarina and Tresephen.

On the ride home, Roger asked Abel why he had stopped him from speaking.

"I didn't think we should tell them the real reason yet about going to the deserted mines. Usually tradespeople are interested in money before anything else," replied Abel.

"Where will we get five gold pieces?" asked Roger. "Isn't that a large sum of money here?"

"Yes," said Abel. "It is. If Barzillai is willing to loan us that much, I am sure that the Prince will take care of the debt."

"No doubt he will," said Roger. "I am sure he is aware of everything."

The boys finally arrived at the ranch, and though it was late, Barzillai and Simone and Adah had not gone to bed, but had stayed up to wait for them. Simone had saved some food from the evening meal and now served it to the very exhausted boys.

Barzillai was quite willing to help with the cost of the endeavor, and promised to give them the gold coins they needed before they departed in the morning. Then he insisted that everyone go to bed immediately in order to have enough rest for the journey ahead of them.

Roger fell into a deep sound sleep promptly, but towards daybreak, he began to dream. In his dream, he came to a mountain and he knew somehow that there was a mine inside although nothing revealed this on the outside. It was as if he had supernatural knowledge about this mountain and what it contained. He heard a voice speaking within his self, and the voice said, "I reveal many hidden things; I know what deep darkness holds, though I live with light. Look for the cleft in the rock under the cover of a shadow. No bird of prey can be seen on that hidden path, and no lion can be found there. The roots of the mountain are laid bare, and through the tunnel in the rock, your eyes will see the hidden treasures. Find the source of the river and bring the treasures into light."

In his dream, Roger looked at the mountain carefully and as his eyes roamed upward, about halfway up he saw a dark place under a jutting rock ridge, like a shadow under a ledge.

He woke up startled and as soon as he felt calm again, he got up and found a writing tool and paper and wrote down all that the voice had told him.

He was confident that it was the Prince who had said these things so distinctly in his dream. After he dressed, he put this paper in the pocket of his clothing. Abel was awake now, too, and Roger told Abel and then Barzillai about the dream. Barzillai listened carefully to the details of the dream, and also felt that it was direction from the Prince.

"But I still feel that it would be wise to employ a guide," Barzillai said, and he gave Abel a small leather pouch containing the five gold coins.

Adah also had something to give to Roger and Abel. First, she handed a small bag containing the black gunpowder, to Roger. Then she showed both of the boys a small hollow reed, two tiny arrows, and a small vial of some substance.

"This is a blow-dart weapon," she told the boys. "And the liquid in this bottle is a very potent juice from the midnight flower. One drop on the tip of the dart can cause a man to remain unconscious for almost a day and a half. Be careful; don't use it unless you absolutely must."

They went outside, and Adah showed them how to use it, and they practiced until they knew how far to stand from the subject they wanted to strike, and how hard to blow into the reed.

Then it was time for breakfast, and they ate together with Barzillai, Simone, Adah, the shepherds and groomsman. Roger and Abel treasured that meal with them, for they did not know when they would have another such meal together with their friends.

Yet they were eager to leave and begin the search for their two missing friends. They had decided to go on foot, so that the horses would not be left unattended for long, while they explored the hidden mine. They knew that Adah and Tobias would take good care of them in their absence, though both boys would miss their equine companions.

Adah walked with them to the road which would take them into the town. She had some final words to say to Roger and Abel: "Do not forget who you are, and to whom you belong. You will be tested---but not beyond what you can endure. Remember the promises he gave you. To underestimate yourself is to underestimate the Prince."

So Roger and Abel walked away with that admonition burning in their hearts. Roger had seen the face of the Prince that morning in the gold book of promises, and it had stirred his heart. He felt the love of the Prince compelling him on this journey, and he knew that the Prince was with them, though they could not see him.

Abel was puzzled about something; and as they were walking further down the road, he asked Roger what he thought about it.

"How could people think of the Prince of Grace as someone evil?" Abel wondered.

"It's like there is an enchanted mirror," said Roger. "The one who is truly evil uses deception and causes people to see the Prince of Grace as evil. And now I realize that they also see us as evil, too." Roger told Abel about his experience when he was captive to the evil prince.

They reached the town, and went immediately to the tavern. The door was open, though the place seemed deserted. The brooms were right where they had left them, so they picked them up and swept the side of the room they had not done the night before. There was no sign of the bartender, so they put the brooms away and went up the stairs.

Everything was quiet up here, as well. Abel tapped lightly on the door of Tamarina and Tresephen's room, but there was no response. Abel and Roger waited, not knowing what to do. At last, the door opened slightly, and Tamarina said through the door: "Did you bring the money?"

"Yes," said Abel. "I have it, and I will give it to you when the journey is complete."

Tamarina frowned, and then replied, "All right. Give me a moment." She closed the door, and Abel and Roger waited.

Finally, the door opened and Tamarina and her husband emerged. They were not dressed in their colorful gypsy costumes; their clothes were brown and drab like dirt and sand colors. They both were wearing trousers, loose shirts, vests, and hoods with cowls. Their brown boots were dusty and creased from wear.

Tamarina suggested that they go down through the back entrance. This was a narrow door at the end of the hallway that Roger and Abel had thought was a supply closet, but instead it opened to a very dark and narrow winding stairwell. The stairs ended at another narrow door which led outside.

From here, they began their hike through an open wilderness beyond which loomed the mountain range. Now Roger and Abel understood why Tamarina had dressed as she did. This plain was dotted with sticker bushes and juniper trees with sharp needles. The ground cover was like tall yellow grass stems, dry and brittle in the red-brown dirt.

The mountain range just ahead was checkered with ridges and ledges, and Roger wondered to himself just how hard it would be to find which ledge was the right one.

When they arrived at the base of the mountain in front of them, there was a protruding part just in front which was shaped like a stalagmite pointing upwards. There were many such formations scattered all throughout this mountain range.

Now they came to a group of these which looked like the fingers on a hand. Tamarina and Tresephen climbed up beside these and went behind them; here the path led into a fissure which opened up into a canyon. They proceeded through the canyon with its twists and turns until it ended and the trail led upwards.

Now they were at a level on the side of the mountain where there were many jutting ridges and ledges with shadows beneath the overhang. The sun was high overhead, and the shadows were dark. Tamarina looked around her, shading her eyes, as if she were trying to recognize something. Roger noticed this and felt a cold shudder, even in this hot sunlight.

Chapter 29

Tresephen climbed to a shadowy ledge and after checking for signs of snakes, he sat down in the shade, and drank from his canteen. The others followed him and rested in the shade. As it was noon, Abel and Roger unpacked their sandwiches. Simone had made enough for Tresephen and Tamarina and they were grateful for the food. They all finished eating, but they lingered there in the silence of the mountain, saying nothing themselves.

Then Tresephen spoke for the first time in a language Roger and Abel understood. "It is ....hard to.... find," he said slowly, turning his eyes upward as he struggled with the words.

Roger followed the direction of his gaze and looked at the maze of ridges and overhanging ledges. Suddenly, he felt a surge of confidence and he stood up and looked carefully at the ledges. In his mind, he saw the ledge in his dream, and instantly he knew which one it was.

"I know which one it is," he said with assurance.

"How?" asked Tamarina in disbelief and incredulous.

"I saw it in a dream," he answered.

"You are a psychic, then? A fortune teller?" she asked Roger.

"No," he said. "I know the Prince, and he gave me the dream to guide me."

"The Prince of Grace is real?" Tamarina asked in surprise.

"Yes, he is," said Abel, "And that is why we are here. He sent us."

"I have heard of him," said Tamarina, "but I thought it was just a story---you know, a bedtime story."

"We are here because the prince wants people to know that he is very real, that he loves them, and that he has the power to help them," said Roger.

Tamarina turned to Tresephen, and a torrent of words in their language came pouring out of her as she explained to Tresephen what Roger and Abel had just said.

Roger looked at Tresephen, and it almost looked as if there were tears in the man's eyes. He said something to Tamarina in their own language.

Tamarina translated to Roger and Abel, "He said that it sounds almost too good to be true, but if it is true, he would like to meet this prince."

"Then you shall," said Abel. "Either we will take you to him, or he will come to you."

Tamarina explained to Tresephen what Abel had said, and his joy at this showed in his face.

They all stood slowly, knowing that the next part of their journey might become very dangerous. "Do you have lanterns?" asked Tamarina anxiously.

"Yes," said Roger, for Barzillai had equipped them with lanterns and extra candles.

Then they began to climb up to the ledge which Roger had seen in his dream. Tamarina looked in and exclaimed, "This is it! Your dream is true."

Abel dug in his supply bag and pulled out the bag of coins. He held it out to Tamarina, saying: "You have fulfilled your part of the bargain. Here is the money."

Much to Roger and Abel's surprise, Tamarina declined the money. "No," she said. "We did not help you find it, your Prince did. We cannot take your money."

"But you led us to the right place in the mountain," protested Abel.

"There is something going on here that is more important than money," said Tamarina. "I don't know if it is fate, or what you would call it, but we were supposed to help you----maybe it is because of this Prince."

Roger had a sudden inspiration. "Come with us," he urged. "Maybe we will need your help inside the mine, as well. Do you know your way inside?"

Tamarina hesitated. "It has been a long time since I saw it." She spoke earnestly in their language to Tresephen; he looked down for a moment at the ground under their feet, and then he looked up at Tamarina and nodded. "We will go with you," Tamarina said.

Roger and Abel were overjoyed and thanked Tamarina and Tresephen. Then Tamarina said, "Before we go in, I think you should tell us what we are looking for. This once was a mine, but all of the copper is gone now. There are no treasures here....so what are we looking for?" she asked.

"Lost people," said Abel. "The Prince has sent us to look for those who are lost."

"I must warn you," said Tamarina. "It is easy to get lost in these tunnels, and never find your way out again. You would die in the darkness. We must stay together, and protect our lights at all costs."

They all tightened the straps on their shoulder bags to secure them more tightly to their bodies, and then one by one, they lay down on their stomachs and squeezed through the narrow opening in the side of the mountain.

Once they were inside, it was pitch black. All of the outside noises were shut out---the birds' singing could not be heard, the sound of wind or rain could not penetrate, the sound of flying insects was silenced. It was another world inside the mountain, one in which they could not see. At least they could hear each other's voices, and what a relief that was. They touched each other's arms in the darkness and said something just for reassurance.

Tresephen knelt and fumbling in his bag in the dark, he managed to find his tinder box and began striking the flint pieces together. Tamarina found her candle and knelt beside him. When the candle was lit, their faces showed the extreme relief they felt when they could see again. Their expressions were eerie in the candlelight, but even so, it was a welcome sight.

They put the candle in the protective cover of a glassed-in box lantern. No sudden draft of wind could blow the precious flame out, since it was secluded by the glass container. But they knew that their time was limited to the few hours that the candles would last.

At least they could stand up here in this tunnel, but when this one ended, there were three different tunnels branching from it. Now Roger could see that this was like a maze; it was a labyrinth. Tamarina pointed out symbols that had been carved at the top of each tunnel opening; these were meant to aid the traveler if one could remember them.

Roger looked at the symbols carefully; there was a bird of prey, a lion, and a simple drawing of what looked like roots. Suddenly, he remembered the dream, and he took the paper out of his pocket. "Tamarina," he said. "I need to read this paper close to the light." He squeezed closer to her as she held the light up for him to read.

"This is what I remembered just now from my dream," said Roger. "The voice of the Prince said that no bird of prey can be seen on that hidden path, and no lion can be found there, and the root of the mountain is laid bare."

They stood there thinking about this, and looking at the symbols, and then Abel understood. "The right path to take is the one with the root," he said. "We need to avoid the one marked with a bird of prey, and the one marked with a lion. That's what it means."

"And I think we will be going down," said Roger. "There must be an underground river, and that is where the hidden treasure will be. The next part of the message said to search the source of the river and bring the treasures to light."

Tamarina explained all of this to Tresephen; and then he took the lantern from her, and he went first into the tunnel marked with a root, and the others followed behind him.

Roger could feel that they were on a descent down into the underground. It was getting colder and damper as they went. The tunnel wound around and around and there were small openings in the walls here and there which might lead into even other tunnels, but they did not investigate. The light made grotesque shadows on the rock walls, but at least they did not see rats or centipedes or other creepy creatures down here in the depths.

There was a sort of low "roar" in their ears; it seemed to be caused by the depth of this hidden underground world. Roger remembered seeing pictures of the catacombs under Paris, and it reminded him of this---yet this seemed even more remote from civilization. There were no paintings on the walls, and certainly no parties down here. He almost seemed to feel the weight of the world above him----and then he heard another sound.

Chapter 30

The sound still seemed far off, but it was the sound of water. Now there were many tunnels branching off of the one they were in; at each intersection they had to listen carefully and choose the one in which they could hear the sound of water.

Every turn brought them closer to the sound which gradually became more distinct. The first candle in their lantern had burned low, and they had to replace it with the second. Now there were three candles left. All wrong turns at this point might cost them some of their precious light, so they were extremely cautious in their choices.

Since so much depended upon listening, there was not much room for conversations between them, yet their comradeship was growing nonetheless. This was a great benefit derived from being forced into a tense situation together. They communicated more by expression instead of words, and found they could understand one another.

Roger's revelation from the dream confirmed him as the leader of this expedition as far as decisions to be made, yet each person felt equal through acceptance and respect. Roger's confidence did not come from this role, but through the presence of the Prince that he felt was with their little group. He received a much needed courage and calm from this presence.

And so they proceeded through the tunnels until the sound of the water grew louder. Now they were very close to the source, and they were much deeper underground.

The tunnel turned sharply and opened up into a large room with high cave walls. It was as if they were now standing on a balcony and looking from a height of three stories down over a pool of water within a very large cavern. There was still a low rock wall extending from the tunnel, so that they could hide from sight if necessary by crouching below the wall.

There were rock formations surrounding this underground chamber, with many ledges and natural steps leading down to the water, which was a dark aqua blue color. Flaming torches on poles were placed all around this pool of water and there was no need of their feeble candle light here. Other than this, there was no sign of human occupancy.

Manmade steps led down from where they were, to the level of the naturally formed steps in the piles of rock around the pool. Water was flowing out of this lagoon toward other lower parts of the cavern, so it must be flowing in from the other side though they could not see this. They would have to make the descent to find the source of the river.

With the strictest silence, they began the climb down the manmade steps, and then down the natural ones, taking the utmost care not to kick any loose rocks accidentally. Their tedious descent was grueling but necessary, for they knew that the splash of even one small rock would echo loudly in this cavern. At the same time, they were listening carefully for the sound of human voices.

Once they made the descent, they discovered that there was a narrow tunnel pathway leading out of the large chamber, alongside which the river was flowing into the water of the pool. Just before the tunnel opened into another large room on the side of the river, they heard human voices. The sound was distorted and unnatural, but it was definitely human.

Hardly daring to breathe, they crept closer to the sound of those voices, and at last they were able to peek into this other cavern. The sight was horrifying, but there was still cause for rejoicing, for within the group of people imprisoned in a large metal cage, Roger and Abel saw their friends Kamaris and Deonsel.

Their captors were not in the cavern, so the four searchers continued on the path out of the tunnel, trying to stay in the shadow of a ledge. Their own shadows betrayed them; the light from the torches around the cavern revealed their shadows on the wall. The prisoners made no sound; perhaps they realized from the stealth of those entering that they had come to free them and not to harm them.

The flowing river separated them from this prison, but there was a footbridge across the river. While they waited in hushed silence, trying to decide how best to free the prisoners, Tamarina whispered that Tresephen could pick the lock on the cage.

The river was flowing in from the other side, but it was a darkened area, so they did not know what else could be in that direction. They did know what was behind them, so it was decided that Roger and Abel would watch for danger coming in from the side of the river's entrance, and Tamarina and Tresephen would release the prisoners and head back the way they came through the tunnels. "Once you are free," Roger warned, "Do not wait for us---keep going."

Once they were out of the tunnels, these captives could escape into the woods and they would all meet up with Adah at Barzillai's ranch. Abel and Roger knew that Adah could guide them back to the Kingdom of Grace. Tamarina and Tresephen would be free to choose; they could go back to their tavern and be musicians again, as long as the captors did not see their faces---or they could go to the Kingdom of Grace with the others.

These instructions were whispered to Tamarina, and then the four of them crossed the bridge. Tresephen immediately began tinkering with the lock on the cage, and Abel and Roger stood guard, watching the dark entrance of the river way. The prisoners were silent, but their eyes were pleading and their hands reached to grasp at Tamarina, who stood close by. She motioned to the captives to remain silent.

It was a very tense moment while Tresephen struggled with the lock and then at last it came open. Tamarina quickly whispered instructions to the captives to quietly follow her, and then she and Tresephen led the way back across the bridge, and back to the pathway through the tunnel. They retraced their steps back into the large cavern. Roger and Abel waited with rapidly beating hearts as this little procession marched past them.

They waited until all the captives were safely through the tunnel and in the next cavern.

Suddenly, they saw approaching peril; there were lights in the darkened area where the river came in. The lights were still far away, but they were there. Roger instantly knew what he had to do; he reached for the bag of gunpowder hidden in his shoulder bag. He would have to seal off the entrance to the large cavern room, so that no one could pursue the captives.

He had seen something lying on the ground in the big cavern room, and he had picked it up. He remembered from the science book at the school that this was a "safety fuse" used by miners to blast through rock with black powder. Abel looked at Roger holding this fuse and his eyes grew wide.

"If you explode that, and seal off the entrance on this side, we will be trapped," said Abel urgently. "I know," said Roger, in deep consternation over this decision. "There is not enough black powder to explode the rock in a larger space," Roger explained. "It has to be a much smaller area to seal it off," he said. "The narrowest spot in the tunnel is the obvious place."

"If you are sure that the Prince means you to do this, go ahead," Abel said grimly.

Roger went to work; he tried to remember everything he had read in the science book. He filled the tube in the fuse with the black powder, placed this in a deep narrow crevice in the rock wall, and covered it with damp sand retrieved from the river bank. He found a piece of a stick by the river in debris left by the water, and used this to tamp down the sand over the gunpowder.

The fuse was only long enough to light it from the side on which they were on; they could not risk lighting it while in the tunnel. Once it was lit, they would have to get as far away as possible---which meant crossing the bridge to the other side of the river.

Roger looked up and said in his heart to the Prince, "I trust in you," and he lit the fuse in the flame of a torch. Then he and Abel ran across the bridge and took shelter behind the cage and close to the rock wall behind it.

The blast shook the room and rocks crumbled and fell on the pathway in the tunnel, blocking the opening to the big cavern room. Dust from the crumbling rocks filled the air, and would have choked them, but Abel had dipped some cloths into the water and they had held these over their faces as they waited for the blast.

The entrance to the large cavern room was sealed. On the other side, all of the escaping people were by now up on the "balcony" of the room, but they saw what happened and knew that Abel and Roger were doomed---they could not escape. Tamarina and Tresephen did not allow the people to stop and ponder this; they kept them moving. They would not allow the sacrifice of their friends to be for nothing; they must press through and get to the woods.

The blast was heard by whoever carried those lights in the dark area of the other entrance, and those lights were moving more swiftly in the direction of the cave chamber that held the now empty cage, and two young men who waited with hope mixed with dread.

Chapter 31

They did not have to wait long; the pursuers appeared with lanterns in hand and fury in their eyes. Their leader appraised the situation with steely cold glares and quickly two of his henchmen moved to apprehend Roger and Abel. These two jerked the boys to their feet savagely and held knives to their throats.

The leader of this band of men stepped forward. "Don't kill them yet; I must be recompensed in some fashion for my loss of slaves to trade, although I hardly think the two of them will compensate my loss."

"And what did you hope to gain by closing the tunnel, my little saboteurs?" said the tall man in his insolent mocking manner. "It can just as easily be opened again."

The two boys wisely said nothing in reply; no retort would have helped matters at all.

"Take their bags and lock them up for the night," said the leader. "I'll deal with them in the morning."

The two ruffians took away Roger and Abel's shoulder bags, shoved the two boys into the black metal cage, and locked it with the same lock as before.

"Now let's see how you get out of it this time," said the leader in his derisive tone. Then he and the others left the cavern.

The boys lay down on the floor of the cage, which was actually the cave floor. It was cold and damp, and a very unpleasant place to sleep. Yet they were so exhausted that they began to get drowsy. Several of the torches began to sputter, and the flames were shrinking as these torches began to run out of fuel. Roger was relieved to remember that Tamarina had the remaining candles in her supplies, and Tresephen had the lantern.

Finally they fell asleep in the darkness, and when morning arrived, they could not even tell it had come. Only one torch remained lit in the cavern room.

"Roger," said Abel in a low voice in the darkness. "They didn't take everything. I still have the blow gun and the darts and the sleeping drug, hidden in my clothes."

"Oh," said Roger in amazement. "I'm glad you thought to do that. But guess what? I have something even better---(and here he chuckled)---I hid a gold book in my shirt!"

Abel laughed too, he was so happy to hear this news.

Suddenly, they both heard a voice coming out of the darkness; they heard a rustling and a clinking of metal. "How can you laugh?" said the voice.

"Who are you?" asked Abel.

"Only a slave," said the voice bitterly. In a few moments, the flame of a torch flared up again as this person refueled it, and Roger and Abel saw that it was a girl. Both of her ankles had a metal ring circling them, and a short chain between these rings made her walking difficult.

The girl slowly made her way to each unlit torch and after lighting them again, she turned to go back out the way she had come in.

"Wait," said Roger. "How did you come to be a slave?"

"I was stolen, just like the others you saw in the cage," said the girl. "But Pagano kept me as his personal slave."

"Do you want to be free?" asked Abel.

"There is no way I will ever be free. He keeps a close watch on me," said the girl sadly.

"What if we could free you?" asked Roger. "Would you come with us?"

The girl hobbled closer to them to speak in a lower voice. "Pagano would kill me if I tried, just as he will kill you if you try to get away," said the girl. "I would rather be a slave than dead."

"What is your name?" asked Abel, and the girl answered that her name was Sahara.

Roger looked at her in the light and saw how physically beautiful she was. No wonder this Pagano kept her for himself, he thought. Roger felt something he had never felt before, but it made him uncomfortable and he tried to quell it. He knew it was not love; it was only a selfish desire. He remembered what Adah had said right before they left; she had warned Roger to remember who he was, and that he would be tested. He knew instinctively that these strange feelings could not be trusted, since they were not based on the promises of the Prince.

The basis of these feelings did not originate from his trust in the Prince; they came from some kind of greed which was trying to capture his heart just as surely as this metal cage kept him within its trap. The girl came even closer, and Roger felt his heart beat faster. She said in a soft and sympathetic voice, "I am so sorry that you are in here. If there is anything I can do to help you, I will try," she promised, and then she turned and hobbled away, disappearing into the darkness.

Roger let his breath out in relief, and Abel turned and looked at him in surprise. "I don't think she is trustworthy," said Abel. "Don't tell her anything about us or any of our plans."

"Why would she be wearing those leg-irons?" asked Roger in confusion.

"Just to make us feel sorry for her," said Abel. "I think she is using her charms to trick us."

"I hope she didn't hear the secrets we said just before we noticed her," Roger said with concern in his voice. "I am so longing to hear from the Prince---a message, anything."

"Well, let's read from the gold book," suggested Abel, and so they did.

It was hard to read the words since the torch light was not very close, but some of these promises they had memorized, which made it easier to read the words on the page in the dim light. Their hearts were encouraged and cheered by the sincerity and goodness in his promises; there truly was no one with such trustworthy character as the

Prince. This strengthened them and renewed their courage and hope.

They would certainly need that for the events of this day.

Pagano and his men came into the cavern, unlocked the cage and dragged Roger and Abel out of it. Pagano's henchmen tied Roger and Abel's hands behind them and then pushed the two boys toward the dark area leading out of the room. And it was here that Roger and Abel discovered the source of the river; it was at the edge of this cavern that the river flowed out of an underground spring.

Roger and Abel thought of the people they had set free; these captives undoubtedly were the treasures brought to light. Roger and Abel were both happy and satisfied that they had accomplished the Prince's mission.

Now they found themselves walking through another long tunnel; there was a pathway alongside the spring and going beyond it. The tunnel had many twists and turns, and they knew with each turn that they were ascending. Finally, they came to the end of the tunnel and far ahead they saw a very welcoming sight: daylight.

They emerged blinking at the sudden change of light, and squinting in the brightness of the sunshine as their eyes adjusted. As things came into focus, they were dismayed at what they saw. There were wooden stocks not far from where they were standing, and Pagano told his henchmen to lock Roger and Abel in the stocks until he had decided what to do with them.

The boys stood in the hot sun for hours, each with his head stuck through a hole in the stocks, and their hands stuck through holes to the right and left of the hole for the head. Just when Roger thought he would pass out, Sahara came with two goblets of water. At first, Roger wondered if it could be drugged, but he was too thirsty to resist, and when she held the cup to his lips, he drank it all. Abel did as well, with the other cup.

Then Roger noticed that Sahara didn't have the leg irons; this time she had iron rings around her wrists with a chain between them. "Where are your leg irons?" Roger asked her.

"Pagano gave me some freedom today," she answered. "If you cooperate with him, he will treat you better. He told me I could bring you some water, and I also asked if he would release you from the stocks---see, I am keeping my promise to help you if I can."

The henchmen came just then, and released the boys from the stocks and they had a few minutes to stretch their backs after their hunched position. Then the henchmen made them sit down at the base of a tree trunk, and bound them tightly to the trunk before walking away.

They were all alone (Sahara was gone, too) when suddenly a white dove flew down to them.

Chapter 32

The dove landed on Roger's shoulder, and its soft
wings brushed against his cheek. He could not
stroke it, or touch it at all, since his arms were
tightly bound with ropes against the trunk of the
tree. Abel was in the same position.

So the dove hopped down to the ground close to
Roger's hand, and Roger noticed that there was a
small tube attached to the dove's foot. He was
able to wiggle his fingers and to remove the tiny
tube from the dove's leg, and to open it. There
was a bit of paper rolled inside it, but the writing
was so small, and he could not bring it closer to
his face to read it.

So the dove picked up the note in its beak, and
returned to Roger's shoulder, holding the paper
close enough for Roger to read the message,
which he read aloud so Abel could hear. The note
said: "You will go to trial, but do not worry about
what to say. I will give you the words. Remember
how I trained you." The paper was signed "Sir
Guide".

The dove flew away with the bit of paper in its
beak, towards the mountain ranges in the east
which they had crossed seemingly so long ago.

And after a while they could no longer see her, but they knew she was headed back to the Kingdom of Grace, for this was Serena, the messenger of Sir Guide.

This was the confirmation that the boys needed so desperately at this moment. They knew now that their actions had not been an impulsive mistake, and that they were being lovingly watched over and cared for, even in this vile place.

The wiles of Sahara had much less effect on Roger at this point. No false desire could compete with his satisfaction in the companionship of the Prince, who loved him as a son. So when she came back to bribe him to leave the services of the Prince and join with Pagano, whose pay was far more lucrative, he was ready with a response.

"Why do you stay with Pagano?" Roger asked the girl. "You know what he is, and that he enslaves people and sells them."

"He gives me everything I want," answered the girl with a toss of her head in defiance of any conviction over wrong doing. "Does your Prince do that for you? I don't think so."

Roger looked straight at this beautiful but deluded countenance. "No, he doesn't. He gives me everything I truly *need*," Roger stated emphatically. "You are the one who is enslaved, but I am free."

"Ha!" said the girl. "I just wear these chains to get sympathy. I am free to do what I want."

"I doubt that," said Abel. "If you don't please your master, you will surely suffer for it, for you *are* a slave. And if someone pleases your master more than you, you will lose all your privileges and you will be nothing to him."

The girl stomped away indignantly, but not before Roger saw momentarily a flash of startled fear on her lovely features. He knew then that she knew the truth of what they had said to her, though she would not admit it. He would not trade places with her for all the gold in the world. Roger had hope, but this girl was living under constant fear and impending doom.

Abel and Roger could see more of the terrain around them now from their place by the tree. They could see the shimmering sea in the late afternoon sunlight; the sun was glinting off the white waves and sparkling on the blue water beneath the surging white foam. There was some type of large provincial building with colonnades and arches; it was made of stucco and looked very airy, as if designed to capture the sea breezes in its courts and porches. On one side of this building, there was a platform and nearby, there were poles set in the ground and each one had an attached chain.

"That was most likely the place for the slave auction," Roger thought to himself. Abel was at this moment, thinking precisely the same thing.

They would find out the purpose for the building in the next few moments, for two armed guards untied them and escorted the boys into this building, where their fate would be decided. They were led, or rather pushed, through the open porches of this building, until they went through two large doors into a stateroom, which appeared to function as a civil courtroom.

Roger and Abel were forced to stand between the two armed guards close to the front of this room, where there was a raised dais, and where a dignitary of some kind sat behind a desk. A remarkable calm came over the two boys as they quietly observed their surroundings. There was no fear in their hearts, for they discerned the presence of the Prince, though he could not be seen.

The attendant of the dignitary announced that the proceedings would begin. Then the boys' accusers came forward; first, it was the schoolteacher who testified of Roger and Abel's civil crimes against the community. He claimed that the boys were advocating a heresy of belief that would result in sedition and cause great disorder and confusion among the community.

The school teacher called forward as witness the boy who had expressed such animosity towards Abel and Roger---the one Roger suspected had been the spy who reported on Deonsel and Kamaris and their involvement with Roger and Abel.

Then Pagano stepped forward and in a very rational manner, declared that these two boys had interfered with justice and set free those who had been tried already for civil disobedience and were sentenced to slavery. Pagano cleverly inferred that the provincial government would be losing revenue because of the interference of these two outsiders, since he would have less to contribute in taxes now that his profit from the slave sales was diminished.

The officiating dignitary glared at the two boys and asked sternly, "What do you have to say?"

"What explanation do you have to refute these charges?" the man asked the boys.

"If we are on trial, sir, for our belief in the Prince of Grace, then we have no need to refute any charges," said Abel bravely. Immediately, there was a gasp of surprise from the people attending this meeting.

"And sir, if we are charged for setting captives free from this man's clutches, then we do not need to give any necessary explanation," said Roger firmly. Again, the observers responded with gasps and surprised looks.

The dignitary looked even more sternly at the boys. "You seem to be intelligent boys, and you would certainly be an asset to our community---in fact, you would be highly esteemed---if you could be persuaded to abandon your false beliefs and abide by our rules."

"You cannot persuade us, sir," said Abel. "No bribe is enough to make us desert our Prince."

"Indeed," said the dignitary in a mocking tone. "Where is this Prince? Will he come and save you now? You are in *my* jurisdiction, and I have the right to sentence you."

"The Prince sees me even though I do not see him now," was Roger's reply.

"What nonsense!" retorted the dignitary. "Nothing is real if you cannot see it."

"Are your thoughts real?" asked Roger. "Is your mind unreal? You cannot see the words you speak---does that make them unreal?"

"I can hear them, so that makes them real," answered the man emphatically.

"I can hear the voice of the Prince in my mind," said Roger calmly.

"Hearing voices, are you?" said the highly annoyed dignitary. "Take him away, he's gone insane with these notions of a Prince of Grace." The man muttered angrily to himself in his frustration that he could not achieve a submissive cowering attitude from these boys.

"Where shall we take them?" asked the guards, trying not to anger the man any further.

"Take them to Galvando!" yelled the dignitary. "They are not fit to be anything but galley slaves." Pagano started to protest, but the dignitary cut him off. "And as for you, Pagano, your tribute remains the same regardless of your losses."

The armed guards took Abel and Roger away to a waiting ship in the harbor outside this building, while Pagano fumed and gave the boys the very blackest of looks as they departed. They were relieved to be removed from this man's company, but their relief was short-lived when they saw the ship and its pirate flag. They saw the oars protruding from the openings on the sides of the ship, and realized what kind of fate would await them as galley slaves.

"Remember your training, Sir Guide told us in the note," Abel said quietly to Roger. "Yes," whispered Roger. "He trained us to sword fight---- and I think I know the plan."

Chapter 33

The boys still stood on the wooden dock; they had not yet boarded the ship. The armed guards stood by them as they waited for Galvando, the captain, to make his appearance. Apparently, he was in no hurry, or was quite used to having the power to make others wait on him. Finally, he came to the deck of the ship and stared at the two boys.

One of the armed guards spoke up and said, "We have two more galley slaves for you."

"From the size of them, I hardly know whether to thank you," said Galvando gruffly. "Bring them aboard. I'll see what they can do."

The armed guards pushed the boys up the ramp and onto the deck of the ship, where Galvando stood with crossed arms, scrutinizing his two new galley slaves. The armed guards retraced their steps down the ramp and onto the dock, and disappeared in the crowd of people bustling around the dock.

"What are your names?" asked the captain tersely, and the boys answered just as briefly.

Roger knew in that instant that he must have courage and act on the idea that was given to him.

"Captain…we do have a skill that might be more useful to you than rowing," said Roger with more confidence than he actually felt at the moment.

"What?" asked the captain in an impatient tone of voice.

"We have been trained in sword fighting and I believe we would be more useful to you in combat than otherwise," said Abel.

The captain narrowed his eyes and looked doubtfully at the boys. "I'll give you a chance to prove that," he said. He beckoned to the first mate, who nimbly jumped down from the stairs going up to the upper deck, drew a sword and leered at the boys.

"Give them a sword," the captain told another deckhand, who promptly procured a sword for the boys. Then the first mate proceeded to fight first Roger and then Abel. Neither of the boys was able to best the first mate, but still they managed to hold their own against him, and the captain was somewhat impressed.

"If you're going to be part of my crew, you have to begin at the bottom and work your way up," said the captain. "Start by swabbing the deck. At 6:00, report to the scullery."

Roger and Abel were only too glad to be picking up mops instead of oars, and they found the mops and began to mop vigorously. Roger quietly asked what a scullery was, and Abel informed him that it was the part of the kitchen where dishes were washed and stored.

So at 6:00, the boys found themselves in a small dark smelly room below deck, with their hands deep in sudsy water, washing the plates, mugs, and utensils used by the crew.

Still, they knew they would far rather be doing this than to be chained to an oar and a bench. When at last they were finished, they were ordered up on deck to be guarded by two crewmen, while the rest of the crew went to the tavern for a last fling before the ship set sail.

The two crewmen who were left behind to guard the ship and the slaves, were not too pleased over their assignment, and grumpily told the boys to swab the decks. Abel looked up in surprise, and one of the crewmen responded crudely. "Shut yer face! I know you done it already. Git to work before I strap yuh," he yelled.

Abel and Roger were careful not to react and quietly went about preparing to "swab" the deck again. They kept a watchful eye on the whereabouts of both men, for they knew they had only a short "window" of time in which to escape before the ship set sail.

They didn't have to wait long; one of the men went below deck and Roger nodded to Abel. With his back to the other crewman, and with Roger blocking the man's view, Abel proceeded to load the blow dart weapon. He carefully put a small amount of the sleep-inducing drug on the tip of the arrow that went inside the reed.

When the crewman turned his back for a moment, Abel quickly aimed and blew the dart into the back of the man's neck. The man turned around in surprise, and his eyes opened wide before he slumped over the capstan, a wooden drum with rope wound around it.

Abel lost no time in preparing the second dart--- and just in time, for the crewman came up the stairs leading to the upper deck. When the man turned and saw his fellow crewman slumped over the capstan, Abel knew he had not a second to lose, and without hesitation, he blew the second dart into the back of this crewman's neck as he had done to the other.

This crewman had a slower reaction to the drug and he turned around in anger, knowing he had been hit with a blow dart. He staggered towards the boys, and then he stumbled and fell facedown onto the wooden deck and lay still.

Roger and Abel looked at each other, wondering what to do next and then Abel remembered the slaves chained below. "The galley slaves!" He exclaimed. "We can't just leave them."

"But how we will set them free in time?" wondered Roger. "We don't know where to find the key to the leg-irons."

Abel stopped and closed his eyes for a moment, and then opened them. "I think the Prince just showed me where it is," said Abel, and he started running down the stairs to the captain's private quarters. Roger followed him breathlessly and saw Abel look around the room until he saw a small metal box, which he grabbed up and opened quickly. The keys were in this box.

The two boys raced down to the galley of the ship and Abel addressed the slaves: "I am here because of the Prince of Grace----he is real, and he has sent us here to help you. He just now showed me where to find the key to set you all free! But we don't have much time."

After that speech, Roger and Abel began unlocking the leg-irons of each man. The men were almost in disbelief that this was really happening, but as the chains came off, they knew it was not a dream. The strongest of them sprang into action and began to prepare to lower the long boats, while others hung two rope ladders down the side of the ship facing away from the dock. When the last man was set free of his chains, Roger and Abel went with him to the deck and watched as the men lowered the long boats and climbed down the ladders over the side of the ship. The men clambered into the two long boats bobbing in the water.

Before they left, several of the men remembered to thank Roger and Abel. One man said, "Tell your Prince thank you for me. I should like to meet him someday."

Roger replied, "He isn't far from any of us. If you ask him, he will come to you."

The man nodded in reply, and disappeared over the side of the ship. The men began rowing away, heading to the next port to escape into another life that did not include slavery.

Roger and Abel looked in the direction of the tavern, and sensed that time was running out. They straddled the side of the ship, swung their legs over and quietly went down the rope ladders, and then slipped into the water. Abel let go of the keys in the water and they began to sink, while he and Roger began to swim away to the cove nearby where there was a small beach and a line of trees. They hoped to make their escape here and return to their path leading home.

They were grateful now for the swimming lessons they had had with Nate, and they made it to the shore of the cove. Quickly they disappeared into the trees, but then went back and used leafy branches to brush away their footprints on the beach. As they pressed further into the woods, they suddenly stopped in surprise----there was a wooden canoe hidden here. The boys looked at each other in wonder---and cautiously went closer to the canoe. Suddenly a figure sat up in the boat, and Roger and Abel almost yelled in fright, until the person said in a familiar voice: "It's me---it's Adah."

Roger was so happy to see her that he almost hugged her, but he refrained out of courtesy. "What are you doing here?" he whispered. "I thought you would have taken the people we freed back to the Kingdom of Grace!"

"Do not worry," said Adah. "The Prince sent my father to aid them, and he sent me here to help you. You cannot go back the same way you came."

"We are going in this?" asked Abel.

"Yes," said Adah. "We will follow the streams and rivers, and carry it when we have to, over land. That's why it is made to be so light weight."

"We'd better get started," said Abel. "I don't think we have long before it's discovered that all the galley slaves are gone, too." And just then, they heard a great commotion at the ship; they heard shouts and cursing and lights were flaring. They didn't wait to hear any more.

Chapter 34

The night that Abel and Roger rescued his son, Demas Merlono was tortured and fitful. He tried to sleep, but his tossing and turning annoyed his wife, so he got up and went to his office. Finally, he dozed off and fell asleep over his desk, and then he began to dream.

He dreamed that he saw his son and a group of others locked up in a black cage, deep in a cavern in the mountains. Then he saw someone unlock the cage, and lead all the captives out. He saw them walk by in a procession, going through another cavern, and up the steps and out. After that, he couldn't see where they had gone, but he saw someone else. This person had skin the color of melted caramel, long wavy brown hair, and when he turned and looked right at Demas, his eyes were a deep blue like the ocean. His face had some kind of radiant glow, as if light came from within him. He raised his hand and beckoned to Demas and said, "Come, Demas. You must follow me."

In his dream, Demas asked the man, "Where? Where should I go?" The man answered, "Go to the woods in the east and you will find your son. Go now...but you must understand that there will be no turning back. You must not come back here."

"But what about my wife? And my business?" Demas asked in confusion.

"You can ask your wife, but she will not come. Her heart is hard. As for you, you must choose between your business and me," said the man. "Your son has chosen to follow me."

The dream ended, and Demas woke up totally alert with the memory of the dream real and fresh in his mind. He quickly went to wake his wife and tell her of the dream. "Agatha! Wake up!" he urged and shook her gently. "What? What is it?" she asked groggily. "Did Deonsel come home?"

"No," answered Demas. "He is not coming home. I had a dream, and I know Deonsel is leaving this area so that he can follow the Prince of Grace."

"What? He believes in that nonsense?" Agatha exclaimed.

"Yes….he does, and I do too." said Demas. "I saw the Prince in my dream and he spoke to me. I am leaving here tonight to meet up with our son. Agatha, come with me."

"I can't....I don't believe in that silly tale." said Agatha. "Why would you leave me for this? Why would our son leave us for this nonsense?"

"It isn't nonsense, Agatha," said Demas. "Years ago, I heard of the Prince of Grace, but I turned away from him. He is calling me back to him, and I am not going to make the same mistake again."

"I'm sorry, Demas. I can't go with you. I like my life here; my friends, the parties..." she said.

"You go....find our son. Maybe you can come back later," Agatha told her husband.

"No," said Demas. "This time there will be no turning back. If you feel differently later, please come---I know if you search for the Prince with all your heart, you will find him."

"If he even exists," said his unconvinced wife. "But I won't stop you---and I hope you find what you are looking for."

"Goodbye, my love," said Demas. "I hope you will someday see that he is worth looking for."

Demas packed a few things in a small traveling bag worn over the shoulder, and then he left while it was dark, and headed out of town towards the direction of the woods. He went as quietly as he could and stayed in the shadows of the buildings as he left.

The woods were cool and quiet and dark, but a little bit of moonlight shone through the branches of the trees. After a little while, he thought he heard something, though he could not tell if it was the tree limbs rustling in a slight wind----or if it was the whispers of voices. He kept going, trying not to snap any branches or make noises as he walked.

And then he came into a clearing, which had a tiny bit of moonlight shining down into it---and it was just enough that he could see his son. There was the group of people he had seen in the dream, standing in the clearing. Yet he did not see the two boys who had come to his home searching for Deonsel and Kamaris. Instead, he saw the local tavern musician and dancer. The whole group seemed to be waiting for someone…or something to happen.

Demas went to his son and embraced him and tears began to roll down his face. "I thought I had lost you," he said. "Father, how did you find me?" asked his son.

"I had a dream, and I saw the Prince of Grace in my dream---he told me where to find you, and so I came," said Demas.

"Father," said Deonsel. "I'm not going back there---I can't." "I know," said his father. "And I am coming with you."

"What about Mother?" the boy asked. "I am sorry, my son. I could not persuade her to come with us," said the father sadly. "Perhaps when she is ready, she will come to meet us."

The father looked around at the group of people, which was comprised of many of the missing persons from this area. He asked his son what they were waiting for, and his son told him how Roger and Abel had used the gunpowder to seal the tunnel so their captors could not pursue them. "We were waiting in hopes that somehow they might have escaped," Deonsel told his father. "But we cannot wait much longer; the slave trader will search for us."

Just then, another person joined the group; this man had very brown skin, and jet black hair. He stepped so nimbly and softly that no one had heard his approach. "The Prince has sent me to be your guide," he told the waiting group of people. "We must leave now."

"What about Roger and Abel?" asked a very concerned Kamaris.

"The Prince has a plan for their escape," said the guide. "Do not worry." After this speech, their guide turned and beckoned the group to follow him, and he led them on a path deeper into the forest. Demas saw that the guide had a bow slung over his back, and a quiver over one shoulder, which was filled with arrows. "That is well," Demas thought to himself, as he followed the group through the woods path. "We don't know what we shall meet up with."

Demas walked beside his son, and was grateful for this time together. How absurd that he should have waited until such an occasion as this to walk through the woods with his son! He felt a peace in his heart that he had not felt in such a very long time, that he could not even remember when it was that he had last felt this. It must have been when he was a child. Deonsel looked up at him and smiled. Then his son quietly said, "Father, Kamaris is an orphan. I was wondering….could you find it in your heart to treat her as my sister?"

Kamaris was walking ahead of them just now, and Demas looked at her thoughtfully. "If that is what she wants, yes, I believe I can do this," he said, smiling at his son. "Good," said Deonsel, and he smiled back at his father.

Just then, their guide silently commanded them to stop and to be quiet. The group stood waiting; their guide was listening to something, but no one else could hear anything unusual. Their guide changed direction and left the trail they had been following, leading the group away from the area and into another section of forest. This area had some trees which could be easily climbed. Soon, they saw the reason for their departure; a bull moose was roaming in the area they had just left. If this animal felt threatened, it could become very aggressive, and it was best to stay out of its way.

After a while, the moose moved on, and they were able to return to the trail they needed to follow. Demas marveled at the graciousness of the Prince; though their journey might be long and arduous, the Prince had sent them a guide who could hear and sense the danger they could not. Demas wondered how and when they would rest, and what they would find to eat, yet somehow he felt he was completely safe and cared for by the Prince. And all this because of a dream! What then would it be like to actually meet this personage, the Prince? His anticipation was growing as he pondered this.

The woods were incredibly beautiful at night; the moonlight which filtered in was like a blue haze over the green foliage, softening it with a filmy cloud. The forest had its own whisper in the silence, broken only now and then by a human whisper from the band of secret travelers. They came upon a narrow twisting stream zig-zagging its way through the lush and verdant foliage, and their guide permitted them all to drink from this stream. No one, of course, had any sort of supplies to drink with, so it was a matter of kneeling and cupping their hands, drinking quickly before the water slipped through their fingers. The sight of the gurgling water, flowing so freely through the forest, somehow brought refreshing to their minds as well as quenching thirst. At last their guide led them to a place to rest, in a well-hidden cave.

Chapter 35

The canoe glided smoothly through the river water, making patterns of circles in the current around it, in the moonlight. The dip of their oars in the water, alternating on each side of the canoe, made a synchronized sound as if the water was softly clapping in rhythm.

Other than this, it was still and quiet, with only an occasional hoot of a night owl in the woods alongside the river. Adah maneuvered the front of the canoe and guided it skillfully, and Abel and Roger followed her lead. Once, Roger saw a curious deer staring at them from the river bank before it disappeared into the forest.

He felt the Prince speaking to him in this great silence around him, for all this beauty was created by the Prince and his father. Yet none of it could take the place of Roger's yearning to be back in the palace of the Prince and to walk with him in his garden. He wanted to be in his arms again and look into those wonderful eyes of love.

The Prince was yearning for him, too. "Roger, I am waiting for you to come home to me," he said in Roger's mind. "And the captives will all be set free when they know me. Your work will not be in vain."

Through all the hours of traveling, it was this yearning that kept him going when he was exhausted and hungry and so weary of the wilderness and its loneliness. They carried the canoe aloft when the rivers ran toward the west, and they had to change direction. They had skirted the red cliffs and given them a wide berth, though this was a much longer route than the one they had traveled before.

They were now well past the valley in which Barzillai's farm was found, and Roger wondered if he would ever see his horse again. The thought of abandoning Starlight---or of Starlight feeling abandoned---made him sad.

When they took shelter in a cave for a time, Roger mustered the courage to ask Adah about their horses, for she had last seen their condition. Perhaps there was some plan, he hoped. Adah didn't know if there was or not, and she was sad about Marrona, too, so Roger declined to mention this anymore.

As they were trekking through this dense forest, which was a dark green in the absence of much sunlight, they heard the sound of swiftly running water. The sound was magnified from under the birch wood canoe they carried over their heads. They followed the sound until they found themselves standing on a short rocky precipice looking down over a small lagoon. The waterfall cascading down into this aqua blue pool had neither great height nor width, but it was still a rare and beautiful sight. There was sunlight here; it glinted off the white spray.

It had been days since washing, and the blue of that water was irresistible. The three of them left the canoe, carefully climbed down the steep embankment, and pulled off their boots.

They waded into the pool until their clothes were saturated. Adah held up her braid, keeping it from getting wet, for that would take too long to dry. Then they sat on the bank of the lagoon, letting their clothes dry on them in the sunshine. Adah spotted some wild edible fruit and they ate this while they waited, feeling as though they had just had a feast.

When it was time to leave, they pulled on their boots again and climbed up through the rocks to the place where they left their canoe. It was undisturbed, and they hoisted it over their heads and shoulders again. This constant position could become very tiring, so it was not long before they hoped to find another river, heading in the right direction.

At last they did, and this river had a surprise for them; it ended in an estuary---a place where a river meets the sea. They found themselves on a beach close to the sea, though far away from the harbor of the mining town.

The beach was a welcome sight, as it stretched out in the distance. They set the canoe down and looked around; like a serene pastel painting, the light tan of the beach met the light blue of the sky at the horizon line. There were white birds leisurely flying over, some slowly coming down to peck at something in the sand. The unending lapping of the waves on the shore had a hypnotic effect on the three as they looked at the sea.

Then everything that had been pale blue and cream turned to orange and gold and rose pink as the sun began to set in the west. The children were looking off into the west, and didn't notice that someone was approaching from the east on the beach. It was a very tall someone, and he was leading three horses.

When Roger, Abel, and Adah turned round again, they could hardly believe what they saw. This tall man leading the three horses seemed so unreal that it looked like a mirage in the desert. Then

Marrona whinnied as she recognized Adah, and the other two horses could barely contain their excitement at seeing their owners.

Sir Guide (yes, it was him!) kept walking toward the three children who stood "frozen" in their wonder. Roger was the first to react, and he ran toward Sir Guide and hugged him fiercely. Then it was Abel's turn and he hugged Sir Guide just as tightly. In the meantime, Adah had buried her face in Marrona's mane, and had her arms around the horse's neck.

Starlight kept nudging Roger while he embraced Sir Guide, and so he let go of one and held the other, speaking softly into Starlight's ear, as he used to do. Abel's horse Sunrise was demanding his affection, also, and so he turned to her and rubbed her face the way she liked.

It was a glorious reunion that day on the beach, as marvelous as if the sea breeze had just picked up Sir Guide and the horses and delivered them to the children. (I have no idea just exactly how Sir Guide accomplished this feat, but he always did such surprising things. So we should just expect as much.)

Sir Guide had also brought with him the boys' armor and swords which they had left behind in

Barzillai's stable. Now he explained the plans; they were to follow the coastline for a ways.

Then they would again go through the hills, woods, prairielands and moors, finally arriving at their destination: the Kingdom of Grace. Sir Guide also had fresh provisions for the children in their saddle bags---enough for the rest of their journey.

Sir Guide requested a private consultation with Adah, although her horse insisted on remaining at her side, and Sir Guide did not mind. Sir Guide wanted to alleviate any concerns Adah might have been feeling about her father and the group traveling with him, and Sir Guide assured her of their progress and safe travel. The group of former captives would be moving more slowly since they were on foot, but they were even now on their way to the Kingdom of Grace.

The three children hugged Sir Guide once more and then mounted their horses. The horses were prancing and eager for a run on the beach. Roger looked back at Sir Guide who had picked up the canoe and was carrying it on his back; Sir Guide had promised to take care of it. Then Roger and Abel and Adah gave their horses the lead, and they took off at a gallop down the windy beach beside the flowing waves. Roger looked back once more, but Sir Guide was no longer there; there was no trace of him or the canoe.

The shadows were deepening, and it was getting dark, but the horses were enjoying the cool sea breeze and put their noses into the wind. Then the moon began to rise above the horizon of the sea, and the light shone out over the water.

Roger never forgot how it felt to ride Starlight down the beach at night, with her mane and tail blowing in the wind, and the mist of salt water flying in his face as she ran.

At last, the beach ended, and they were heading into the woods away from the sea.

They found a large secluded cave and brought the horses in and made a small fire to keep them safe through the night, though they knew it was really the Prince who did that for them.

The next morning, they continued their routine of reading in their gold books. Sir Guide had supplied Roger and Abel with new ones, as Roger's was lost when they "jumped ship" and Abel's had been confiscated by Pagano. Abel secretly hoped that somehow, that book might have made it into the hands of the slave girl, Sahara.

After all their experiences, these promises of the Prince were more precious to them than ever. They packed the books carefully, covered up the fire, and led their horses out into the fresh daylight to start what they hoped would be the beginning of the end of their journey.

And so it was; they passed through several forests, and rode over many hills that day. That night, they slept in another cave---an even larger one---but Roger hoped it would be the last cave he would have to sleep in for a very long time. There were no skirmishes with wild animals, except for a chance encounter with a wily fox which tried to steal their food.

All day they rode through the high grasses and moaning wind of the moors, and then their eyes filled with tears when at last they glimpsed the turrets of the Palace in the distance.

Chapter 36

Roger, Abel, and Adah did not expect such a jubilant reception as they came closer to the glistening white castle. Their arrival caused a great flurry of activity, it seemed, and the three weary travelers were in a daze at the commotion aroused by their return.

They felt as though they were renowned heroes returning from a great war, as the shouts and hurrahs surrounded the three on horseback. People were running here and there, and waving at them, and their exuberance was thrilling but a bit overwhelming, too.

As they rode up to the castle grounds, it seemed as if everyone in the village and from within the castle itself was on the lawn to greet them. There were banners flying and flags waving everywhere they looked, and children were laughing and jumping up and down with excitement. It was a spectacle to behold, and Roger and Abel looked at it all in amazement.

But the one face Roger so wanted to see was not in the crowd. His eyes searched everywhere, but he could not see the Prince. He tried to remain jovial and grateful for all the appreciative attention, but his heart was heavy with disappointment. At last, a very tall figure came walking towards him--- Sir Guide was here!

Sir Guide came close to Roger as he sat on Starlight and spoke with great kindness. "Roger," he said, "Don't be dismayed. I know you are looking for the Prince---he isn't here yet, but when he comes, he will be looking for you. He has missed you very much."

Roger was able to smile again at that assurance and waved a return greeting to all those who were demonstrating joy in their return. Sir Guide walked alongside them as they approached the walkway. Here, the Prince's groomsmen came to take their horses and care for them. Roger, Abel, and Adah gratefully dismounted and turned the reins over to the Prince's servants who led the horses away to the stables.

Abel's mother and father and siblings came rushing over to him then and embraced him. Then each member of Abel's family hugged Roger and then Adah, as well. After that, Abel's family walked with the trio up to the castle entrance and Mercy welcomed them in.

Sir Guide dismissed the crowd, but invited them all to come back for the celebration they would have in a few days.

Sundae and Saphire were waiting just inside the castle, and as Roger entered, Sundae ran and flung herself into Roger's arms. He picked her up and twirled her around, and then setting her down carefully, he noticed all the decorations she and Saphire had put up for their welcome home.

"Do you like it?" Sundae asked, and her face was beaming. "Yes, I do, Sundae! It's beautiful," said her brother with true appreciation for his sister's enthusiasm.

Adah admired the signs and decorations, too, and Sundae shyly hugged her.

In the meantime, Abel's parents were anxious to take their son home again, and Abel's sisters threatened to kidnap him if he didn't comply! So laughing, Abel allowed himself to be dragged away by his sisters.

Saphire took Adah and Sundae to the girls' rooms, and Roger was left alone with Sir Guide. "Roger," said Sir Guide, "I think when you see why the Prince is not here, you will be very encouraged. I would tell you, but I know he would rather that you see for yourself."

"Oh," said Roger. "Then I will look forward to that time."

Sir Guide put his arms around Roger in an embrace and Roger held onto him, too. Finally Sir Guide released him, and they walked together to Roger's room, where there were clean clothes for him to change into, now that he would finally have a chance to bathe.

For the next several days, Roger, Abel, and Adah rested and ate, and rested some more and ate, and rested again. Their bodies needed time to recuperate from all their exertion, and so did their horses. The groomsmen took care of their horses magnificently, and Adah was so pleased to see how well Marrona looked when she checked on her.

Abel came once a day to the castle and shared a meal with his friends, but his family was so starved for his company that they would not part with him for more than this.

Finally one morning, a messenger ran into the castle with a great shout, "He's coming!" And oh, what a great deal of excitement there was then, and bustling about in the castle and out on the grounds. Roger tried to stay out of the way, as he was still very tired, but anticipation was fermenting in him as he observed the preparations and realized what it meant.

Then amid the sound of many shouts, Roger looked out the castle window facing west and saw an impressive sight. He tore out of the castle and joined the crowd filling the entire castle grounds with rejoicing residents of the Kingdom of Grace.

There was a troop of travelers approaching, and out in front of them, a resplendent figure donned in silver armor and helmet was leading them. At his approach, there were the sounds of many trumpets, and a great shout arose from the watching people. Roger saw that there were many brilliantly colored banners hanging down the sides of the castle from the parapet. The heralds who blew the trumpets stood upon this parapet, and others waved flags from this height.

Below them, the royal guards of the castle stood at attention and awaited their commander in chief. A thrill went through Roger at the sight of this warrior, for he knew it was the Prince.

Close by the warrior walked a man whose complexion and clothing were so similar to Adah's that Roger knew immediately this must be her father. And then he began to recognize the faces in the group of people who were being led so triumphantly by this mighty warrior.

It was the captives; the Prince had gone himself to escort and lead them to his domain.

Such was his grace, that he would lead them himself out of the land of their captivity. Roger saw Deonsel and Kamaris in the group, and he was happy. Then to his surprise, he saw Deonsel's father accompanying him! There was Tresephen and Tamarina; they had chosen to come to the prince and leave their old life behind, and Roger was glad.

The other captives Roger had not had time to become acquainted with, but now that they were here, he was sure that he would be able to.

The group approached the castle walkway, and the warrior stopped. He unsheathed his silver sword and raised it high in a salute; his royal guards responded by returning the salute and their swords gleamed in the sunlight.

The warrior returned his sword to its sheath at his side, and continued marching forward. Every one of his subjects bowed low in reverential love of their sovereign prince.

Roger knelt on one knee and bowed low before this mighty warrior, whose presence he yearned for. At the moment, though, he knew the concern of the prince was for these who had been newly rescued from great evil. They would need his compassion.

And so the procession went past him, though Roger noted that the prince saw him in the crowd and nodded ever so slightly to him as he passed.

When all of the former captives had been cared for, and lovingly welcomed into the estate of the prince, and the crowd had dispersed to their homes, Roger waited expectantly for a glimpse of the one he loved so dearly.

It was late afternoon by then, and the sun was beginning to set. Roger stood looking out upon the Prince's garden, hoping for their reunion. Then he saw what he longed for; the prince entered his garden, and Roger ran to meet him.

I don't think you could view that embrace without tears in your eyes, when Roger ran into the arms of the Prince. There were definitely tears in Roger's eyes, as the Prince held him close. Neither of them said anything for a time, and then they sat down and the Prince had his arm around Roger's shoulders. Roger leaned against the Prince and felt his heartbeat.

Finally Roger spoke: "I missed you so much."

The Prince answered, "I longed for you to come home every day…but I was never far from you. I was watching over you, everywhere you went."

"I know," said Roger. "But I wanted to be here, with you."

"You are my son," said the Prince. "I will never be far from you. I will never desert you. Everywhere you go, I will be with you. Do not doubt my love for you."

Roger looked into those deep blue eyes, and he believed.

Chapter 37

The next day, preparations began for a great and momentous occasion: the ceremony for all those who followed the Prince out of captivity.

Adah and her father were still guests at the castle, since their presence was requested at the ceremony. Adah, Abel, and Roger were given new clothing just for this ceremony.

When everything was ready, the golden doors were opened to the throne room and all the guests were ushered in. The room was absolutely glorious in honor of this event, and everyone looked around in wonder.

Yet as always, the most wonderful aspect was the Prince himself, dressed in his royal clothing with his golden circlet crown atop his dark wavy hair. The light emanating from his face reflected his joy at this rescue that had been accomplished.

When everyone had arrived, the Prince stood, and there was a roar of praise for this great and mighty sovereign, who loved his people so much. Then he gestured for silence, and the room became so silent that you could almost hear your own breathing.

Roger was so in awe that for a moment, he felt as if he couldn't breathe. Sundae was next to him, and she looked up at him and squeezed his hand. She was grateful for her brother.

Then the Prince spoke and one by one, he invited each of the rescued persons to step forward and receive his antidote, if they had not already had this privilege. When it came to Demas' turn, the Prince told him how glad he was that Demas had returned to him.

Demas looked down in remorse, but the Prince assured him that all was forgiven, and after he received the antidote, he would be made new. Demas touched the prince's scepter, and a brilliant light surrounded the throne. When Demas turned round again and looked out at the people, his face had a glow that made him look ten years younger.

"Welcome home," said the Prince and embraced Demas. "We will recover lost time," the Prince told Demas, who was speechless from the effect of the antidote, but nodded happily.

Deonsel and Kamaris were the next ones to receive the Prince's antidote, and they too had no words to say except a very grateful thank you to the Prince of Grace. The glow of ecstasy on their faces revealed all that they were feeling in that moment.

Tresephen and Tamarina came after them, and received the Prince's antidote with great anticipation and awe, and they were not disappointed in the tremendous change they felt immediately. The light was beaming out of their faces, and they hugged one another, and then each in turn embraced the Prince of Grace.

Roger and Abel stood watching as each of the others that they had released came forward.

These were overcome with elation at their freedom from captivity, and they were overjoyed to be in the presence of the one who had arranged their rescue. Some had already received the antidote before captivity, while others were longing for this deliverance from the disease of sin. Each person was formally adopted and welcomed into the Prince's family as his heirs.

On their way back to their places, many of these people who Roger did not know yet, came over to Abel and Roger and thanked them for all their endeavors to set them free.

After all this had taken place, the Prince called Roger and Abel and Adah to step forward. When they were standing before him, the Prince looked at each of these young people with such love and joy in his eyes, that they were mesmerized by his gaze.

Then he spoke: "Adah, my daughter, you excel in so many ways, but most of all you excel in following my ways and I am so proud of you. Thank you for your bravery to help in this rescue." The Prince set a silver tiara with golden jewels on Adah's black hair, which had been braided with shimmering gold strands woven into it. Then the Prince gently pulled Adah close to his side and wrapped his arms around her, and kissed her on her hair. All the while, Adah hid her face in his clothing, but when he released her and she stepped down, all could see how much she loved the Prince and how happy she was that he was proud of her.

Next, the Prince beckoned to Abel to come closer. The Prince described parts of their mission and what the two young men had experienced, and how they never gave up or lost their resolve throughout the mission. The Prince placed a gold circlet crown, similar to his own, on Abel's head, and then he held Abel in an embrace for a long moment.

Abel stepped down, and then Roger came close to the throne. The Prince again told of the difficulties that these young men had faced valiantly, and how they persevered, even risking their lives and freedom to help those who were slaves. The

Prince also placed a gold circlet crown on Roger's head and took Roger in his arms in an embrace.

The three were still standing there and had not yet gone back to their places, and the Prince stated again how proud he was of his children who had faithfully completed this mission. Then there was thunderous applause from the audience, and Adah, Abel, and Roger were so engulfed by this tremendous sound that for a moment Roger felt transported to an even higher place than this. He closed his eyes, and then was almost afraid to open them; he felt if he did, he might be looking at the Prince's Father.

When the uproar died down, the Prince began to sing to his children, and this is what he sang: *"This day I found you, and made you mine; you are my children, forever mine. Your heart is precious, and joined with mine; I gave my blood to make you mine. And all eternity, I want you near; I love your face, for you are mine."*

And as he sang these words in his rich voice, and the notes floated out over them, there was healing in this song---wounded hearts were healed from many hurts as he sang.

Sir Guide then ended the ceremony with a blessing-prayer.

After that, there was a procession of people out onto the castle lawn, where there was a reception. White covered tables were adorned with platters of delectable food, and there was a special table for all of the newcomers to sit with the Prince.

After the meal, Cedric was looking for Roger, and took him aside for a while. "I promised you I would tell you the story of that black birdcage, and I must keep my promise," he said in a laughing manner. Roger was fascinated to hear how the birdcage incident led to Cedric's eventual rescue, and he especially smiled as Cedric related how he spent time with the Shepherd, never guessing that he was actually in the presence of the Prince.

"Thank you for taking time with me to share your story," said Roger. "Please tell Rusty and Pearl for me that I miss them very much and I think of them often," said Cedric before he walked away, and Roger promised he would.

That jolted Roger; he had not thought of his own world in quite some time. He almost wished that he could forget it forever, but then he remembered his parents. He was still their son, too, and he wondered how it would be when----and if----he went back.

Just then, he was startled by something else; Kamaris came to talk to him, and he was stunned at her appearance. She was radiant, and incredibly beautiful, and his heart was stirred. Yet this feeling was nothing at all like the sensation that had come to him when he saw Sahara. Those feelings had been at war with his allegiance to the Prince, and aroused an awareness of degradation. He did not like the way that feeling had pulled at him to respond to it. This was different; it was a respectful admiration for the beauty of a person.

It struck him just then, that this was how Rusty looked at Pearl, and he decided in that moment that he would wait for just such a relationship. He would not expose his heart to the hurt and harm caused by any Sahara captives he might meet in the world.

Just then, as Kamaris walked away, the Prince looked at Roger and their eyes met; the Prince gave a slight nod of approval, and Roger knew that the Prince had heard his thoughts.

Roger had an alarming thought immediately after this; what would he do when he did go back to his own world, and he could no longer see the Prince?

Just as he thought this, the Prince spoke into his mind: "I will always know your thoughts, Roger, because you are connected to me now. And nothing---not space or time, or anything else---nothing can separate you from my love."

Roger spent the rest of that day enjoying the company of his friends: Abel, Adah, Deonsel, Kamaris, Nate, and Rhoda, and Sundae played with Nate's sister Zelia.

That night, Roger slept deeply, but toward morning he began to dream: he dreamed of riding Starlight down the beach at night, when the moon was full and round and cast white light on the rippling waves of the ocean; Starlight was running, and the breeze was blowing against their faces, and he smelled the sea air even in his sleep.

Chapter 38

The next morning before it was even light, Roger got up and dressed. He read in his golden book of promises by candlelight, and then he went outside to the stables.

He saddled up Starlight, and they went riding through the pastures of the Prince as the sun was coming up. It was a glorious morning, and the glowing colors painted in the sky seemed like a banner of love just for him. They slowed to a walk and enjoyed all the beginnings of that morning, and he patted Starlight and spoke softly to her.

He did not know how many more opportunities he would have to do this.

When he came back to his room later to have breakfast, Mercy served it to him. When he was finished, she came again to tell him that the Prince wanted to see him in the garden. Roger went down immediately, and went inside the gate. There stood the Prince waiting for him, and Roger's heart felt as if it were enlarged from the love he felt when he saw him. The Prince turned and looked at Roger, and Roger never forgot that look. There are no words to describe the love that he saw in the Prince's eyes.

Roger had a feeling that he knew what this meeting was about, and he took a deep breath.

"Come," said the Prince. "Let's sit down and talk."

So they sat together on the white carved benches by the water fountain and the Prince waited a minute before he said anything. There were cardinals darting in and out of the trees, and hummingbirds were sipping from the large lilies across from where they sat. Those unusually large butterflies were flitting past them and around them.

The tiny chickadees were singing, and every now and then Roger saw the brilliant hues of the blue bunting among the green of the foliage around them. The sun made sparkles on the water of the fountain, and there were glimpses of rainbows over it. There was something lovely and refreshing in this remarkable place, everywhere he looked.

At last the Prince spoke. "Roger, it is time for you to go back to your home," he said gently.

Roger sighed. "I had a feeling you were going to tell me this," he said sadly. "Is it today?"

"No, tomorrow," said the Prince. "I want you to have all this day and night at least to be with your friends---they will want to tell you goodbye."

"What about you?" Roger asked. "Will I ever see you again or come back here?"

"You will learn to know me in your own world," said the Prince. "I have a different name there, but there is a book of my promises, and I will speak to you."

"I can't leave yet," said Roger. "There is one thing I don't know--something I have to find out."

"What is that?" asked the Prince with a slight smile, because he already knew what it was.

"The ancient secret," said Roger. "You told me I would find out what it is, but I still don't know."

"You have found it," said the Prince and his eyes twinkled. "You just have not realized it, because you are thinking of it as some ancient magic spell."

"Then what is it?" Roger asked in bewilderment. "Don't keep me in suspense, I have to know."

"It's me," said the Prince. "I am the ancient secret---everything that you need is in me. Now that you know me, you have everything you need. All the treasures of wisdom are found in my promises because they are my words."

Roger sat there, pondering this, amazed that the truth was so simple and yet so profound.

The Prince went on to explain that Roger's time here had been like a parable for him to understand the Kingdom of Grace. He said, "You must go on looking for me in the mirror of my promises. That is where you will see my image, and be transformed into my image."

The Prince went on to warn Roger that he would encounter the enemy in his own world, too. "Remember that the enemy wants you to look into his warped mirror and see yourself as worthless and stupid and unable to do anything good; but when you look into the mirror of my promises, you will have confidence that you can help other people."

"How would I do that in my world?" Roger wondered.

"You can speak the truth that will set them free from lies," said the Prince. "Lies bring insecurity and fear, but truth gives confidence and courage. Lies bring guilt and shame that makes people into slaves. Only my love can help people feel truly valued," said the Prince.

"What about the antidote?" asked Roger.

"There is a reality of this in your world, because it is the only thing that heals sin," said the Prince very solemnly.

"I wish I could take my horse back with me," said Roger.

The Prince laughed so merrily that Roger couldn't be sad and laughed with him at the thought of it. "Perhaps you will have a horse later in your own world," said the Prince. "It would not work out just yet."

"Thank you for letting me have her for a while at least," said Roger gratefully, and the Prince smiled.

Later that day, Abel and Roger raced their horses in the open field, and Starlight won by a mere "hand's-breadth" as Abel called it, so they had to race again, and that time they tied. They left it at that, since all their friends wanted to go swimming together one last time before Roger would have to leave. They all knew by now that Roger was leaving, and the Prince had also spoken to Sundae.

Sundae was not as sad as Roger thought she would be, since she had begun to miss their mother, and Roger was relieved. He was the more reluctant of the two of them. How strange to think that he had been the resistant one at the beginning! Now, he could barely accept the thought of going away from the Prince. So much had changed in himself that he did not feel like the same person.

When he mentioned this feeling to Sundae, she said, "That's because you're <u>not</u> the same person. Remember? When you received the antidote, the old you died and you became new. That's how the antidote works."

And she was right---this was true. And the Prince had said there was a reality of this in his own world. He had to discover how, and he was sure the answer was in the book of promises. That would be the first thing to look for when he returned home.

There was a great banquet that evening, and Roger and Sundae sat by the Prince, and all their friends sat at this table also, for they could not bear to be parted while Roger and Sundae were still here. Adah was among the friends sitting with Roger. She had not yet returned to her home; she had remained at the castle since it was the Prince's request.

Now she understood why he had asked her; she too must say her good byes. And all of those who Roger and Abel had helped to set free were sitting close by. Each one of them thanked the two young men once more, for their service to the Prince which had brought them freedom.

Demas especially expressed his thanks to Roger and Abel, for without their intervention, he knew he would not be there with his son. He and Deonsel and Kamaris were going to stay at the castle for training in the service of the Prince. Tresephen and Tamarina were learning the songs of the Kingdom of Grace under Sir Guide's tutelage, and would be part of the Prince's band of royal musicians.

After the meal, these musicians performed a ballad commemorating the deeds of the Prince when he gave his life to rescue his people, and they sang of the healing power in his blood. Then there was a beautiful dance performed by a group of young girls led by Saphire, and Sundae was enthralled with this. She whispered to Roger that she hoped to do this herself one day, and Roger was happy at the thought.

The evening was ended with a dazzling and elaborate fireworks display out on the castle lawn. Still, no one wanted that evening to end, and so Sir Guide accompanied Roger and all of his friends to the Prince's garden, and allowed them to talk together a while longer. They sat by the water fountain and reminisced about all they had gone through together. Then they parted for the night, knowing that the final goodbyes must be said in the morning.

Chapter 39

It will be hard to describe that morning---for it was exquisitely beautiful. It was more beautiful than all the other mornings, Roger felt, and his heart ached with the sorrow of leaving it.

Mercy brought the clothes they had first arrived in, to Roger and Sundae. That was such a strange feeling to put them on again; these clothes seemed to belong to someone they had known a long time ago in a very distant memory.

They had breakfast with all their friends in the Prince's garden, and it was delightful. The air around them was so clean and pure, and the sky so blue without any tinges of gray.

Then the Prince arrived, and walked with Roger and Sundae and all of their friends back through the castle, through the great arched doors, and onto the walled corridor. As they began their descent down the brick steps, many people followed them out of the castle. There were many already who were waiting on the lawn to wave goodbye.

When they came to the stone walkway, the Prince stopped and told Roger and Sundae that from here on, their friends could not come. He would accompany them himself for the rest of the journey back to the garden where they had arrived that first day in his kingdom.

That was the hardest part; Roger and Sundae hugged their friends one last time, and thanked them all and Sundae especially hugged Saphire. They looked out at all the people they had come to love, standing on the lawn of the castle, and waved farewell.

Then they turned and began to walk away, and it was so hard for them to do this that the Prince began to sing to them. Sundae took his hand as he sang: "I shall never forget you, wherever I am; you are my friends and my love. No one can take up your place in my heart, for I promise my favor is yours. As the sand has no number, and the stars have no count, such is my unending love; and though the world ends, and the mountains should crumble, your fate remains firm in my hand."

"Oh, that one is beautiful," said Sundae. "I love that one especially."

"Then sing it with me," said the Prince, and he started singing again, stopping and starting as needed for Sundae to learn all the words and melody.

"Roger," said the Prince. "I need to hear your voice, too."

"I'm not much of a singer," said Roger apologetically.

"Yes, you are," said the Prince. "You're part of my family and we're very musical. You need to try. Sing for me," he urged.

So Roger did, because the Prince asked it of him, and as he sang he felt more confident.

The Prince began to sing with him, and suddenly Roger could hear a harmony and began to sing in harmony with the Prince. The Prince looked at Roger in delight, and Roger smiled back.

"When you get back home," said the Prince, "and you begin to feel lonely, sing for me, and you will feel close to me. I will be listening."

"And you, too, Sundae," said the Prince, and he squeezed her hand.

So they sang together all the way back---through the farms, the border of evergreen trees, the golden fields, across the little bridge over the singing brook, through the woods with the leaves that chimed, and along the pathway leading to the first garden.

Then Sundae had a curious thought. "How are you going to send us back, since we came here through a mirror?" she asked the Prince.

Roger was so busy enjoying this last walk with the Prince that he had not even thought about it enough to be curious. But now he too was intrigued with the dilemma.

"Oh, I have many surprises," said the Prince, with laughter in his voice. "And I don't like to do things the same way all the time."

So Roger and Sundae knew they would have to wait and see what the Prince planned to do as his surprise to them. They only hoped that they could spend a little more time with him.

They arrived at the first garden, and the Prince said right away, "Let's sit down and talk for a while. I don't want you to go back just yet." (For of course he knew how they felt.)

So they sat on the white cloth and wood chairs amidst one of the circles of flowers. This time, Roger could look around and really admire this garden with its hues of red and blue in the trunks of the trees and their green and orange leaves. Sundae couldn't help but run over to hear the flowers laughing when the bees touched their petals. Then she came back to her seat and looked steadily at the Prince. He was still the most beautiful part of this place.

She looked up at him, and said, "I love you." And light began to shine from his face.

Roger sat looking at this phenomenon and he remembered when he had first seen this; it was when he first began to really love the Prince. "I love you, too," he said. "Thank you for everything you have done for us---and most of all for changing us through the antidote in your blood."

And now the light was becoming more brilliant and even his clothes began to radiate light. "You are my son and my daughter," he said to them, "because you accepted my antidote. Your world is very dark because of the disease of sin, but my promises will be your light."

When the Prince stood, they knew they would be leaving him soon, and they clung to him. The Prince held Roger in his arms, with Roger's head on his shoulder, for a few moments.

Then he released Roger and held Sundae in his arms. She had her arms around his middle. Then a little breeze began to blow, and it moved the green and orange leaves and fluttered the gold lacy stuff draped on the trees. It almost sounded like a sigh.

Sundae lifted her head and looked up at the Prince, and he nodded. It was time.

With his arm around Roger, and holding Sundae's hand with his other hand, the Prince guided them over to the well. "What do you see?" he asked them.

Roger looked and Sundae leaned over and looked at the water in the well. As they stared, slowly they saw an image forming on the water---it was of the little antique store.

"It's Rusty and Pearl's shop," he answered. "It's the inside of it," interjected Sundae.

"When you touch the water, you will go home," said the Prince. "Rusty and Pearl will be waiting for you, so don't be afraid."

"But….isn't there a souvenir or something we could bring home?" asked Sundae wistfully.

"No," said the Prince. "But don't be sad. I have sent gifts ahead of you, and you will find them when you get home."

"Oh," said Sundae cheerily. "Thank you so much!"

The last things that Roger and Sundae saw were the light in his face and the love in his eyes, as they touched the water, and then the next things they saw were the faces of Rusty and Pearl.

The brother and sister found themselves in front of the antique mirror, and Sundae was standing on the stool which was still positioned below the mirror.

"How was your adventure?" Rusty asked Roger, looking at him with a knowing kind of gaze.

Pearl helped Sundae down from the stool, and gave her a hug. "Thank you," said Sundae. "Thank you for helping us to go on this adventure."

Rusty said, "It's getting late. I'll close the shop, and we can bring you home in our car and you can tell us more about your adventure."

"That would be great," said Roger.

"Wait, before we go I need to give you both something," said Pearl. "These packages came today, addressed to the shop but with your names on the address label."

Roger opened his package and smiled. It was a pair of stirrups. Pearl looked puzzled and asked if Roger had a horse, and he just smiled and said, "Not yet."

Sundae opened hers and found a pair of dance slippers. Pearl remarked that they looked a little large for Sundae, but Sundae said confidently, "That's okay. They're for the future."

Chapter 40

Sundae and Roger climbed into the back seat of Rusty's vehicle, and Rusty and Pearl sat in the front. After Roger gave directions, Rusty backed out of the alley parking area and the car began moving through the streets towards Roger and Sundae's home.

It was quiet in the car for a moment; suddenly Rusty and Pearl spoke impulsively at the same time, then stopped abruptly and laughed at themselves.

"What happened?" Roger repeated Rusty's question. "There is so much to tell."

"What was it like?" Sundae repeated Pearl's question. "Absolutely beautiful---but the Prince is the most beautiful of all. He healed us with his antidote."

Pearl turned around to look at Sundae and smiled with such joy at this news. "Yes, he is so wonderful," she replied.

"I didn't trust him at first," said Roger. "The evil prince tricked me into following *him,* and I almost became his slave, but the Prince of Grace came to rescue me."

Pearl looked expectantly at Roger, to encourage him to keep telling what happened. Rusty couldn't look back, because he was driving, but he was smiling as he listened.

"But I didn't know it was the Prince of Grace, because he came as the shepherd. I was still angry with the Prince because he let Sundae go to the castle, and not me. I didn't understand what was going on. So I lived with the shepherd for a while, and I began to love him so much that I wanted to stay with him forever," said Roger.

"I already felt like that," said Sundae.

"He asked me to go to the castle, so I said I would, and there I found out I had been with the Prince of Grace all that time because he loved me so much. Then he healed me and adopted me," said Roger as the words tumbled out of him in a rush. "After that, Sir Guide began to train me. We learned all kinds of things."

"Like riding horses?" asked Rusty, still looking at the road, but glancing in the rear view mirror to catch a glimpse of Roger's face.

"Yes! We did," answered Roger, and Rusty could tell how much Roger had enjoyed that.

"I learned how to swim," said Sundae happily. "And one night the Prince danced with me."

Pearl looked at Sundae with such a far-away look in her eyes; you could tell she was remembering special things from her growing up years in the Kingdom of Grace.

"Then the Prince sent me on a mission," said Roger. "My friend Abel and I went together."

"I couldn't go," said Sundae. "But Saphire kept me company so I wasn't lonesome."

"Oh," said Pearl. "Isn't she the kindest person!"

Sundae definitely agreed, and Roger began telling about their mission.

"We started out on horseback, and then the Prince sent us a guide---a girl named Adah. She knew the wilderness really well, and I don't know what we would have done without her. So we made it to this man's farm and started going to a school in the town nearby. It was against the law in that place to talk about the Prince of Grace, but we did anyway---secretly---but someone found out and our friends from the school were kidnapped."

Roger kept talking hurriedly because they would soon be at his house. "So we went to go look for them, and found some people who knew where they might be. They were being held prisoner way down deep in a deserted mine. We got them out---and the other prisoners with them---and then we met up with Adah again, and came back to the Kingdom of Grace. But the escaped people went with Adah's father on foot. Sir Guide had brought our horses back to me and Abel and Adah, and we came back a different way."

Sundae got very animated and excited and started telling about that last part of the rescue. "You should have seen it when those people came to the Kingdom of Grace. It was so exciting! The Prince himself was leading all the captives out of the wilderness, and he was wearing his silver armor and his silver helmet and he had a silver sword! There were trumpets blowing and flags waving and people were shouting praises for the Prince."

"I wish I could have seen that," said Pearl and her eyes were shining.

Just then, they drove up to Roger and Sundae's house. It was a small gray, slightly dilapidated, plain house with an unkempt yard in a neighborhood of similar houses. There was no light on, so Pearl assumed that no one was home.

"Will you be okay?" she asked Roger.

"Yes, we will be fine," said Roger. "What was the promise you told me long ago?"

Pearl smiled and quoted it. "I will always be there for you; you can depend on me forever."

"Well," said Roger as he got out of the car. "Now I know the one who said that."

"Wait…" said Rusty, before Roger began to walk away with Sundae. "Can you come and see us tomorrow after school? We would like to hear more, if you don't mind….and we'd really enjoy your company."

"Please?" Pearl said with a plea in her voice.

Neither Roger nor Sundae really needed much coaxing to respond to that request, and they promised to come to the shop the next day.

And they did; Roger and Sundae were at the little antique shop without fail, immediately after school was finished for the day.

Rusty and Pearl were delighted to hear more details about their trip to the Kingdom of Grace. Rusty laughed so hard when Roger related how Cedric told him the story of the birdcage, and Pearl and Rusty were so happy to hear greetings from their old friend.

(Dear reader: The story of the birdcage can be found in The Angel in the Garden, where you will meet Rusty and Pearl when they were children)

Roger and Sundae came back again the next day when school was over, and visited with Pearl and Rusty. But on the third day since they came back from the Kingdom of Grace, Pearl and Rusty were waiting eagerly for their visit, but Roger and Sundae did not come.

They did not come back the next day or the next, and Pearl said, "Something must be wrong." Rusty agreed, and as soon as it was time to close the shop, he suggested that they go back to Roger's house and make sure that he and Sundae were all right.

Rusty and Pearl said nothing to each other as they sat in the front seat of the car and Rusty drove back to Roger's house. Something definitely looked strange, Rusty thought, and he pulled the car into the driveway and got out of the car. So did Pearl, and they went to the door and knocked. There was no answer. Then Pearl peeked through the window of the door and could see into the house. It was vacant; there were no belongings left in the house that she could see.

"I think they've gone," she said sadly to Rusty. He moved to another window of the house and looked in. The room was completely empty; there were no furnishings or anything left.

With a sense of desperation, Rusty went into the backyard and looked around. It was desolate, and a great sense of sadness started to overtake Rusty.

He and Pearl got back into the car and sat there for a few minutes. Then Rusty turned the key in the ignition and started the car. He backed the car out of the driveway, and slowly drove back to the antique shop. Their apartment was on the second floor above the shop.

Neither of them said anything until they were at home in their kitchen, sitting at their little table. Pearl said, "You know they will be all right, because the Prince will not ever desert us, wherever we go."

Rusty sighed and said, "Yes, I know---and I'm so grateful that they belong to the Prince now. He will take care of them. I'm just sad….I would have adopted them, if I could have."

Pearl smiled. "You know the Prince always has his plans! He doesn't tell us everything he's doing, but he's always working things out."

Rusty smiled at that thought, for he knew perfectly well it was true. "Yes," he said in assent. "But I am surely going to miss them."

Chapter 41

Stored-up memories are a treasured thing, and sights and sounds that cause us to open up our "treasure box" and look at those special memories are a good thing, too.

That is what happened to Rusty and Pearl when they looked at the antique mirror hanging on the wall. They remembered two children who came into their lives one afternoon. Pearl never saw the vision of the garden again in the mirror, but the memory of Roger and Sundae remained a picture in her heart.

One day that summer, while Pearl was away on an errand, the mail carrier delivered two letters to the little antique store. Rusty decided not to read them until Pearl got back, but he was having a hard time resisting the temptation to open them, because one of them was from Audrey. The other letter had no return address, and he could not decipher the postal code to see where it came from.

So as soon as Pearl was back, Rusty brought her into the kitchen and made her close her eyes. "Now hold out your hands," he commanded. "Palms up," he said.

Pearl obeyed and held out open hands, with her palms facing up. She was nervous and excited, not having a clue as to what Rusty intended to put in her hands.

Rusty gently laid an envelope in both hands, and then told her to open her eyes. She noticed the return address on one of them immediately.

"A letter from Audrey!" she cried. "But who is the other one from?"

Rusty shrugged his shoulders and gave her his teasing smile. "It's a mystery."

"Well, I'll read Audrey's first," decided Pearl, setting down the other letter to open the one from Audrey. This is what she read aloud:

Dear Pearl and Rusty,

I miss you so much. I think of our days in the Kingdom of Grace often, and I am so happy we met there. When I close my eyes, I can still see the face of the Prince and his eyes…and it reminds me of how he loves us.

Since we met up again at your shop, I have tried hard to find out where Cornelia could be, but I have not found out yet. But several nights ago, I had a dream and now I know at least what is happening in her life! In my dream, I saw that she has a gardening business---a plant nursery, I think it is called. I could see this place in my dream, and it is filled with many green plants, shrubs, small trees, and flowering bushes. In my dream I saw that on the property where the plant nursery was located, there was an enclosed garden. It had a high stone wall for privacy and a black wrought iron gate, and inside was a beautiful sculptured garden with sidewalks and white benches and trees for shade. There was even a water fountain! And I saw the stone angel----now I know what happened to it.

I am so glad Cornelia has it; I thought it had disappeared for good. Since it belonged to her grandmother, it's a good thing she has a place for it. But guess what? This is the best part: There was a big sign by the enclosed garden that said: PRAYER GARDEN, and I saw in my dream that people were praying there—some were sitting, some were walking around, and a few were kneeling. There was beautiful music playing in the background. It made me so homesick for the Prince's garden, but I was so happy to see this. Write soon!

Love, Audrey

Pearl looked up at Rusty and there were tears in her eyes. "This is such good news," she said. Rusty nodded, but he looked as if his mind was far away in the land they had left.

His focus came back to the present, as Pearl opened the mysterious letter and read aloud:

Dear Mr. Rusty and Mrs. Pearl,

I am sorry we didn't get to say goodbye. We had to move suddenly, because of my father. I didn't get upset, though, this time. I know that the Prince's antidote can heal my father, too, and I am counting on it. We were very sad to move away from you, and I can't give out my address right now, but as soon as possible I will. I will keep writing to you and letting you know how we are doing. We miss you very much.

Love,

Roger and Sundae

Now both Rusty and Pearl had tears in their eyes. Pearl had to hurry and get some tissue, because tears were running down her face. Rusty cried, too. Then he went to get an antique treasure box they were keeping for themselves, and he put both letters inside it.

Rusty said thoughtfully that this had been a great and wonderful adventure, and he wondered who else the Prince would send to them.

Pearl said, "Let's go sit on the sofa."

Rusty looked at her quizzically, but went with her to sit on the sofa in what functioned as a living room in their apartment.

"I have a surprise for you, too, Rusty," said Pearl.

"Do you want me to close my eyes and hold out my hands?" he asked teasingly.

"No, just look at me and I'll tell you," said Pearl.

"Okay," said Rusty, turning more toward Pearl.

"Actually," said Pearl, "You just said the clue."

"I did?" wondered Rusty.

"Yes," said Pearl. "You did. You said that this had been a great and wonderful adventure, and you wondered who else the Prince would send to us."

Rusty just stared at Pearl, perplexed at trying to solve this riddle.

"Well….," said Pearl. "We are going on another adventure----this time it's an adventure of our own."

Rusty still had not guessed the answer to the riddle.

"You see," said Pearl, "the Prince is sending someone special to us….a very little someone."

Rusty's eyes grew wide. "Are you telling me….are you…"

"Yes!!" said Pearl. "You're going to be a father!"

Rusty laughed out of sheer joy, then he held Pearl in his arms, and then he cried.

But these were tears of gratefulness.

ABOUT THE AUTHOR

Teresa Lavergne and her husband Guy worked in children's ministry at their church for over thirty years. Twenty-one of those years, they were on staff as children's pastors and served as elementary chaplains at the church school. They reside in south Louisiana. Teresa and Guy hope to publish more of their children's ministry materials.

Made in the USA
Las Vegas, NV
12 January 2021

15772547R00184